Jet, a Gift to the Family

GEOFFREY KILNER

Jet, a Gift to the Family

illustrated by Mary Dinsdale

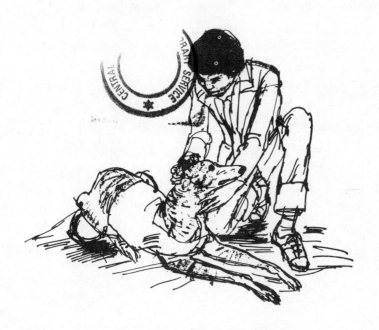

Kestrel Books

KESTREL BOOKS
Published by Penguin Books Ltd
Harmondsworth, Middlesex, England

Text Copyright ©1976 by Geoffrey Kilner
Illustrations Copywright ©1976 by Mary Dinsdale

First published 1976

ISBN 0 7226 5201 1

Printed in Great Britain by Lowe & Brydone (Printers)
Ltd, Thetford, Norfolk

For Joyce, Lisa, Pamela, and Alex

Contents

1   Mrs Reynolds Puts Her Foot Down Gently   9
2   Mr Reynolds Tries to Count His Chickens   20
3   Island in the Sun   32
4   A Singular Event   40
5   Jet Makes a Special Impression   49
6   At the Races   59
7   Beating the Clock   70
8   A Rainy Day   78
9   The Price of a Gift   84
10   Mr Reynolds Takes a Risk   98
11   Under the Weather   107
12   The Midland Trophy   115
13   Lost   122
14   Found   134
15   The Willow Cup   146
16   The Black Dog   154

CHAPTER ONE

Mrs Reynolds Puts Her Foot Down Gently

THEY were quarrelling. Just as he was going to burst in and tell them about the mark he had been given for his English homework, he heard his mother's voice from the kitchen. Her voice was normally soft; now, though she did not shout, she spoke firmly, and the sound travelled all the way down the bare, tiled hall to where David was standing. Disappointed, he waited by the front door, listening for an explanation of their disagreement.

'Where you think we goin' to keep it, an' how you goin' to find the money?'

His mum's voice wasn't angry; she was just being reasonable. David heard only a mumble from his dad in reply; but he knew there was no good answer to his mum's question. Whatever 'it' was, his dad had acted hastily as usual, and was trying to fix them up with something they didn't need, and couldn't afford. Last time it had been a sewing-machine, the time before it was a cocktail cabinet.

'Anyway, you no know nothin' about them, Shirland Reynolds, an' they needs no end of care an' attention. Who you think goin' to spare all that time? I dunno! If somebody wanted for get rid of an elephant I think you'd take him an' expect me to give up me best parlour for him to sleep in. Well I won't have no elephants, an' I won't have this; so you can take it back right away an' tell Earl Campbell that it don't suit your plans to keep it. When you say him goin' home?'

David could wait no longer; his mother's ultimatum made him afraid that 'it' would disappear even before he had had a chance to see it. He went forward down the hall, letting his shoes clatter on the tiles to announce his approach. As he opened the door into the kitchen his parents stopped talking and turned to greet him. He stood in the doorway and gave only half his attention to greeting, the rest he directed to a rapid search around the room for 'it'.

'Hello son,' his dad said, welcoming the interruption, for he knew he couldn't win the argument with words. 'You have a good game?'

'I got "Nineteen out of twenty. Excellent" for my essay about Jamaica,' David said with as much of the dispersed triumph as he could re-muster. He looked at his mum, who followed daily and in detail his progress at the Comprehensive School he had started four months ago. But his mother's look of approval failed to hold him to his triumph; he searched around the room for a sign of what they had been discussing. 'What's dad got?' he asked.

'I tell you what he haven't got: he got no sense. He jus' think we can find money out of the empty air an' buy what we likes.'

'What he bought?' David persisted.

But his mum didn't want to tell him – he knew it. She feared that he would take his dad's side and that she would have two of them to deal with. 'He not buy nothin' we can afford so that an end of the argument,' she said with desperate firmness, knowing the argument had only just begun.

David glanced at his dad and received a broad wink and an eye-signal that 'it' was in the back yard. They were conspirators already. But before he could take the next step and ask his dad about the thing, the door burst open and his sister rushed eagerly in among them. Charlotte was such a demon that she made a sensation at every appearance; the conspiracy could not progress yet a while.

'Mum, we goin' to have lunch? I gotta get back an' play with Jane.' Charlotte gabbled out the arrangements for the next part of her day, and stood impatiently shifting from one foot to the other.

'Where your ribbon? Oh Charlotte! An' look, you gone an' tear your tights, new on today!' Barbara Reynolds looked in despair to her husband, who said nothing. 'An' your coat all mud! You been playin' on that river an' I tell you not I dunno how many times. Take them things off an' let me see.'

David saw that his mum was making too much fuss about Lotty, and trying to stall them. She wasn't sure she was going to win this time, and she was afraid to let Lotty and himself into the argument.

'But isn't lunch ready?' Lotty was plaintive and impatient at once. 'I promise to be out an' Jane gonna be waitin'.' She turned to her daddy – she could win with him without trying.

'You take them things off like your mummy say an' lunch'll not be long,' he told her, and then, though hesitating first a moment, he added, 'We got one more to lunch today.'

His tone was half-fearful, half-joking. And he had

11

reason to fear because Mrs Reynolds said at once: 'Yes, just for today your daddy brought a visitor. But we got room for no more in this family, so it go stay outside till your daddy take it home.'

David took this as his mum's grudging surrender: now he could ask to see. 'What is it, dad? Where?' he asked eagerly, making for the door.

'Daddy, what we got?' Charlotte asked, jumping up and down and tugging excitedly at her daddy's hand.

'Come on then, I show you,' he answered, moving now with a sly half-glance at his wife, 'you come with me.'

'But you remember, you two: it goin' back. We can't afford no unpayin' guests,' their mother told them firmly, even though she knew she had lost.

Outside there was a paved space, bare and bleak. Two outbuildings stood in this yard: a lavatory that was broken and unusable, and a coal-shed that was swept clean and carpeted as Lotty's play-house.

'Here you are then,' their father said dramatically as he put his hand out to open the coal-shed door, 'what you think of this?'

When the door opened a huge creature stepped out slowly and with hesitation, looking at them uncertainly. It wasn't the elephant David had heard his mum talking about, but it was big. Big, that is, for a dog. Yet in spite of its size it seemed delicate. And how shy it was in approaching them – its eyes gentle and sad, its long, slender head so sensitive as it stretched towards them. The dog wore a fawn-coloured coat of felt. It was a greyhound.

'Oh Daddy, Daddy! Is it ours to keep?' Charlotte cried with excitement, and she went down on her knees so that she was smaller than the dog. As she hugged it to her with both hands, David saw the patience in its eyes. Its head, held tightly, was uncomfortable but unprotesting in her embrace. David stroked gently along the curving ridge of the dog's back. From the parts he could see its colouring was black on grey – black brindled, as he was later to learn. And under his hand he felt a trembling, too slight to be seen. 'Cold,' he thought.

It was a raw January day without weather in the shape of wind or rain or frost; but the temperature was low and the cold was numbing. 'It tremblin' with the cold out here, dad.' David looked up accusingly at his father: 'We gotta take it inside.'

His dad pretended to look helpless. 'Your mum say she won' have no dog in the house. Before you come she tell me: "Put it in Lotty's play-house." ' He shrugged and fell silent.

'Oh the poor thing, it want to sit by the fire,' said Lotty, hugging more tightly and spreading her little body inadequately around the dog to warm it. David knew that it was up to him. He went back into the kitchen. 'Mum,' he began, and his mother turned a look of resolve upon him. 'I no havin' no dog here, David Reynolds, so that final,' she said.

'But that dog cold an' tremblin' out there, Mum. If you gonna send him away again it won't hurt none for give him a warm first. You come an' see, he tremblin'.'

'I tol' your dad for take him back. That dog gonna cost five pound a week to keep, an' we no have money enough for keep ourselves.'

'I understand, mum,' David said – it was best to be reasonable with her – 'but if he have to go it don'

13

make any difference to let him get warm first. You come'n see how him tremblin'.'

Reluctantly, Mrs Reynolds let herself be drawn out into the yard. Coming from the house, without being given a chance to put on a woollen, Mrs Reynolds was struck at once by the English cold which she had never learnt to endure. Now it sent a fierce shiver through her frame, and she hugged herself tightly as she stood looking at the group before the play-house.

'Look, you touch him, mum, feel him cold,' David urged.

Following his example she placed her hand flat on the dog's spine, and felt the shiver with which her own thrilled in reluctant sympathy. 'You can bring it into the fire, just for a warm, mind,' she said to her husband, 'but I mean it when me say it have to go.'

Lotty tried to hang on to the dog while her father took it by the collar and led it into the kitchen to the paraffin stove. 'Leave it a bit now, Lotty child, let it settle,' he said, gently.

' "Settle" you say? It not goin' to settle here,' Mrs Reynolds said, reluctant to concede a point. But to fulfil its part in the conspiracy against her the dog did settle, lying in a sprawl before the heat, yet tucking itself in between a chair and the table, a little withdrawn, to shield itself from harassment by the persistent Lotty. 'You have your lunch, an' then you take that dog back, Shirland Reynolds,' Mrs Reynolds ended.

Her husband smiled, nodded sheepishly and sly; but he did not speak, and they all moved to sit down to the meal.

'Where you get him from, dad?' David asked.

'Belong to Earl Campbell, but him goin' back home an' want to find a good owner for his dog before he leave. That dog have won lots of races, lots of money on the track. It called "Allegro", that mean "fast". It a real prize dog.'

'Sure, you don' think you can afford a prize racin' dog, Shirland Reynolds,' his wife said with scorn. 'Why, a prize dog gonna cost you hundreds of pounds. I don' believe that dog ever been near a race-track. Earl Campbell jus' buy it to show off an' then find it cost too much to keep, so he have to sell it for a song.'

'How much did you pay for him?' David asked. 'How much, dad?'

'Cost more than we can afford to pay,' his mother told him, 'even if your dad tell the truth.'

'How much, dad?' David repeated.

'Ten pound down, but look, see!' Mr Reynolds pulled a sheet of folded paper from his pocket and tapped it importantly. 'There, that what gonna count: that dog's pedigree. It tell who its parents are an' ever'thing. See an' look,' he said, opening up the pedigree, but not surrendering it. 'All racin' dogs has their footprints taken jus' like this' – he showed the diagrams of each paw – 'so you can recognize them the same. That a very valuable dog, an' it goin' to win lots of money at the track.'

David was very impressed by the pedigree; he had thought this was just a pet greyhound, but the pedigree showed different. Even his mother stole a glance at the paper in spite of the grunt of scorn she gave at his father's reliance on it.

But now they were seated at table and Mrs Reynolds

15

began putting out the food. 'We goin' to start?' Mr Reynolds asked.

'Yes, it goin' to be cold if we wait. He be here soon, I tell him early,' Mrs Reynolds answered.

David noticed that his mother was immediately less severe when she talked about his brother, Peter. He knew her feeling for Peter, who had left school last summer and hadn't yet managed to find a job. It was a special feeling, because she knew Peter was unhappy and felt a failure, trying to get jobs and being turned down all the time because he wasn't English.

But the simpler problem of Peter's dinner was soon solved. David saw the dog suddenly prick up its ears, and then he heard sounds in the hall. When Peter came into the room, the dog was alert and turned its head around to follow him. David, anxious for Peter to see the dog, kept both of them in his gaze. He saw

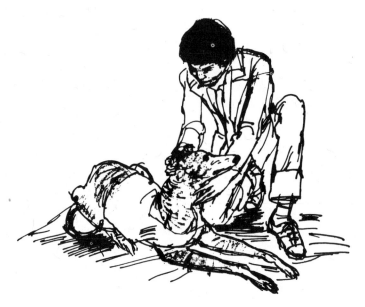

the dog's tail wag, sweeping across the carpet, and he was struck by the interest it showed.

When Peter saw the dog he went straight to it and dropped down on one knee on the carpet. He patted the dog and it stood at once and moved closer to him, its tail wagging briskly. 'You a fine dog!' Peter said with surprise and enthusiasm, 'but you not need that jacket on here. Come on, let see what you really like.' He undid the coat and the dog stood amiably while he was taking it off and smoothing down the black brindling along its flanks. 'You surely a fine dog,' he said. 'What your name?'

'He called "Allegro",' David said, 'a real pedigree dog.'

'Sure, I got the pedigree here,' his father added, producing his paper again like a conjuror – as if taking it out of the air.

'But mammy say that dog haven't to stay here with us,' said Lotty, 'it goin' to cost too much to feed.' She spoke with complaint and accusation, but their mother refused to be drawn. 'Come on, all of you, 'n' eat. The food goin' to be cold,' she said.

But Peter's coming and the new liveliness in the dog were compelling. 'Dad say he goin' to win lots o' races, an' make money for us,' said David, wanting to bring Peter into the argument.

' "He!" ' said Peter with scorn of his younger brother's words. 'That ain't no "he", that a bitch, an' she ain't goin' to win no races yet a while, because she pregnant, man!'

The whole family looked at the dog. 'How you know that?' David asked, unbelieving.

'Well, you can see her all big, an' look here,' Peter touched the dog along the belly, 'you can feel 'em movin'.'

David rose from the table and went to test what Peter told him. He felt a little kick against his hand from inside Allegro's belly.

Lotty was puzzled. 'What he say?' she asked. She didn't like to be left out in the dark.

'He say the dog goin' to have puppies,' her mother told her. And then, turning to her husband, she said, 'You didn't tell me.'

Mr Reynolds looked guilty again. 'I got a paper that tell you who the father is, an' he a pedigree dog too.'

'You mean the puppies goin' to be valuable?'

'Yes, Earl Campbell he say they fetch plenty – fifty pound each!'

'Is that what you pay him for the dog?' Mrs Reynolds asked, the question in a neutral voice that made it harder for him to answer than if she had been angry.

'I pay ten pound down, an' other – ten pound a month.'

'For how many month – four?'

'No, October the last month.'

'A hundred pound!' Everybody was shocked; even Mr Reynolds was struck for the first time by his extravagance. He rose from the table.

'What you doin'? Where you goin'?' his wife asked.

'I don't feel like eatin', I jus' goin' round with that dog, tell him I change my mind.'

'Sit down an' eat.' Mrs Reynolds spoke with mock resignation. 'We can' turn that dog out in the street when she like that. We jus' got to learn to look after her an' hope she have enough puppies to make our fortune.'

Mr Reynolds didn't know whether to be silent and obey, or to protest. The question was too hard for him to decide. He moved about and mumbled; but before long he sat again and tried to hide his triumph.

CHAPTER TWO

Mr Reynolds Tries to Count His Chickens

IF he had as much time as Pete there was no doubt
what he would do with it. Instead of the three books
he now read each week from the library, he would
read six, or even more. Pete was like their dad though,
he wasn't keen on reading. Added to that he seemed
to be depressed by being out of work, so that he spent
most of his time hanging about, either at home, or
around the streets. It was no wonder that their mother
was worried about him; and David could understand
that she had to give his elder brother her special
interest. It was a pity she didn't have more success,
especially in persuading him to read, for that would
occupy his time nicely, David thought.

Yet it was funny when he considered it; his dad,
who didn't normally have time to bother himself with
Pete's troubles, had now offered a solution. Mr Reynolds worked long hours at a mean job in the factory; when he came home he was always tired, and,
though he was naturally a cheerful man and lively, he
rarely interested himself in his children except to ask if
they had been good. But when he had brought the
dog home last week-end it had changed things.

From their first meeting Peter and Allegro had been
very attracted to each other, and Peter, being the
one member of the family who was free from other

responsibilities, had taken charge of the dog and her care. Though he had begun with no knowledge, his natural sympathy had given him a start. David had added to that by reading both the books from the library on greyhounds in order to pass on to Peter all that they said. Now he fed the dog, exercised and groomed it, and, thanks to his father's chance act of providence, he had something of an occupation.

David had read the library books quickly; in part because he was eager to help in doing the best for Allegro, but also because he wanted to have some real books to read. It was a measure of his concern for the dog that he had given over two of his three tickets to it on his last visit to the library.

Now he had those books under his arm, and was hurrying through the gathering dusk to the library. Once through the revolving doors David lost the shyness he felt before the grand front and its imposing stonework. Approaching, even after so many regular weeks of membership, he still felt daunted by the Victorian gravity of the building, just as he had been the very first time.

But inside, in sight of the books, he was much more sure of himself. He would even go quite boldly in among the shelves of the adult library now, when everything in the children's section had come to look too familiar and uninviting.

But tonight was one of those occasions when he found a lot of books that he wanted to read, and he couldn't make his choice. Moving from one book to another, David stayed in the children's library dipping first into this and then into that, trying to decide upon the two he wanted most. When he put one down he hid it behind the other books to keep it safe while he was away. So, he pondered on them as the time slipped by, and in the end he was no nearer to a final selection. He was surprised and alarmed to hear the lady say: 'Will you make your choice now please, the library is closing?'

Waiting till the last possible moment, David chose two of the books almost at random; he had them stamped; and he walked out through the doors into a January night that was cold and wet and dark.

His first thought was for his books, and he stuffed them down inside his anorak, keeping an arm over them against the possibility of their slipping through. Then he set out for home, walking quickly, thinking of the cosiness of his bed and having as much time as possible to read there before the others came to disturb him. Their sleeping arrangements didn't give him much privacy, so David often went to bed very early, especially when he had been to the library and had new books.

To get home more quickly he took a short-cut through 'The Warren'. Even in day-time he didn't like walking through these scarey streets of derelict houses behind the main road. Houses that have been lived in for a hundred years must have their ghosts.

At night perhaps the ghosts roamed. David's scalp prickled as he approached. Why hadn't he kept to the lighted main road? But he had to go down just one street; he could run if need be. Anyway, it was a test, a challenge. When he had done it he would be able to boast.

It was a narrow street he had chosen. The pavement was narrow and its flagged surface was uneven and

22

overgrown. Fear of tripping slowed him down. He stepped into the road away from the window gapes and the gloomy passages that opened a way through to the backyards. But the road was little better, for its surface too was hazardous with loose setts, half-bricks, tiles, glass. Here, he felt the wind stronger too; it frisked him with cold hands, and he could hear it whistling about the house eaves, whispering in doorways.

Hurrying, he forbade himself to look about him, but he kept his eyes skinned. He counted madly to drive fears from his mind. At a hundred he would be safe.

Now he was almost out of the street. He saw the corner ahead that would take him in a few strides out of this haunt of the dead and into the street next to his own, where the houses were so full of living people that there were sufficient to fill all this vacancy.

And indeed, it was they, West Indians and Indians, immigrant families like his own, who had last lived in these mouldering ruins – his dad had lodged here when he first came to England, until he had found another place in which they could join him.

David began to let himself relax as he approached the end of the street, when suddenly he heard a low, mirthless laugh, and footsteps coming towards the corner from out of sight in the other street. He had slid into the shadow of the open doorway of the last house before he was aware of what he did.

In silence, standing, smelling the dankness of the plaster and the decay, he heard the two pairs of footsteps turn the corner, and the low sound of conversation continuing, as two men passed the door

23

opening and turned into the narrow passage which led through to the backyard of the house where he had chosen to hide.

Now he could slip away, turn the corner, and return to the living world and home. But there was something that prevented him; it was an irrepressible curiosity about the two men that fixed him where he stood, heedless of all the reasons that until moments ago had

been urging him away. Instead of flight, David chose to pick his way carefully through the two littered rooms of the house that hid him. His passage was obstructed not only by the piles of rubbish on the floor, but by the huge sag of a lathed ceiling. It hung so low that he had to bend double to pass by it. But he came safely through into the kitchen, and saw through the window that there was a light from a brazier outside in the yard, and that the two men were squatting on their haunches beside it. One of them was side-faced to him, the other presented his back, and David saw long hair hanging down over his shoulders.

Both men were smoking cigarettes, and as David watched, one produced a bottle from his pocket. David saw him uncork it, drink, and hand it to his companion who in turn tilted it at his lip.

'Obeahmen!' David had heard the name so often throughout his childhood. The ideas it conjured had given a shape to fear when he had been alone in darkness or guilty at some misdeed. Now the real shapes of men who fitted the picture appeared before him, and he was rooted to the spot before them with terror. But he was compelled too by curiosity to see what magic they had come here to do.

The men spoke in low tones, so that though David was not ten yards away from them he could hear nothing of what they said. It was clear that they did not mean to start at once, but were waiting, talking idly, and sharing the bottle, either until a certain time, or until someone else arrived. The ordinariness of their behaviour did something to quiet his fear. It allowed his impatient curiosity to get the upper hand, though

25

he barely breathed, lest he should bring upon himself the vengeance of their magic or their knives. He stood chilled, yet unaware of the cold.

David heard the approach of the third man before they did, for the footsteps sounded clearly to him as they passed the front of the house. It was when they went, muffled to David's ears, down the passage to the yard that the men rose and turned to welcome the newcomer. They spoke greetings and the third man replied: 'Sorry me late. Me boy no come home, an' he wanted for to mind the house.'

There was something about the words, even before he recognized the speaker, that had a familiar ring for David. The speaker was his dad.

'O.K., O.K., you pays man,' one of the others said, tolerantly, while the first went immediately to work and started marking out an area of ground, placing bricks that were conveniently to hand to suggest a rough oblong, two yards long, a yard wide.

'Now he ready to start, you take a drink first?' the other man said, offering the bottle to Mr Reynolds. They all three drank and the spokesman said, 'You wants Obeah, he goin' to make it now.'

David had heard of Obeahmen making Obeah, or bad magic, that caused its victims to die. He was shocked to see his dad mixed up with such men, and he couldn't believe that he had come here intending anyone harm.

The man who had made the shape on the ground cut himself off now. Though the others went on talking, he said nothing, and didn't seem to recognize their presence. He stood in the space and at first David thought he was stock-still. But gradually, by slight swinging movements of the man's hair, David realized that he was slowly, rhythmically turning on his hips. His body made circles with a swooning motion that appeared strange and more sinister because David saw it dimly yet dramatically in the light of the brazier.

Now the others were silent, and the movements became faster, the circular motion more violent, until it seemed that the man must shake himself off his feet. His hair stood out from his head and whirled round wildly, and David expected him to go suddenly flying off into space. But at last, when the fury of this motion was dizzying, he gave out a short, sharp cry, and fell abruptly down to lie neatly in the space between the bricks. Without sound, without movement, he lay like the dead.

The other man moved forward a pace towards him and looked down upon the body. 'Obeah! Obeah! Is you there? Man here come want to know somethin' goin' to happen. Me askin' you for him.'

He turned to Mr Reynolds and spoke in a different voice from the priestly tones he had used to Obeah; but, though he noted the change, David did not catch the words nor his dad's reply.

'He have him racin' dog,' the man turned again to Obeah, 'want for know whether him good dog, goin' to win him money.'

There was a groan from the body on the ground, and then a voice that was unlike any voice David had heard before said: 'Black is a gift.' The words were repeated, three times.

'He tell you "black is a gift",' said the priestly one, interpreting unhelpfully, and David was as blankly puzzled as his dad showed himself to be. He did not hear what his dad said next, but the man addressed Obeah once more and said: 'He want to know how many puppy dogs him goin' to have from this bitch's litter.'

'Have jus' as many as him need, an' black is a gift. All done!' said the voice, and there was a stirring on the ground.

'He tol' you all he have to tell,' said the interpreter. 'You goin' to have all you needs an' black is a gift.'

David saw his dad look hesitant as the other held out his hand for payment. He said something humbly and the man said: 'You don' understand now, but it all come clear – you see. You a lucky man.'

Accepting this, Mr Reynolds gave payment, and after another moment of hesitation he turned and walked away, back down the passage and out into the street where David heard his footsteps making for the corner and the peopled world. Though he was anxious at what his dad would say when he came home late David could not leave his place without watching through to the end of the ceremony.

As soon as his father was out of the yard the figure on the ground picked himself up and mumbled something that made the other produce the bottle and hand it to him. He took a long drink, shuddered, and then said: 'How much you take?'

David did not hear the amount named, but he watched as, intently, the two men shared out the money. Then their manner seemed to ease, and, as they fell to drinking again, he knew the ceremony was over. He turned and made his way back cautiously out of the kitchen, ducking stiffly under the hanging

28

ceiling and slipping out through the door into the street.

As he took his first painful steps towards the corner, moving with difficulty from the numbness of such long standing in the cold, he heard the soft sound of one of the men's laughter from the yard. It was a mocking, eerie sound upon the silence, like the deceiving call of some evil bird or wild creature, and David shivered to hear it. Then the two men were laughing together, the second laugh higher in pitch than the first; and the emptiness of the street seemed like a great, bare chamber in which the wind threw the sound about. At one moment it was far away, and at the next it was breathing down upon him. David felt that the shapes of the laughing men might suddenly take substance before him. On the point of drawing himself back in horror from such an encounter, he felt the sound whipped suddenly away.

He reached the corner, and once there he broke into a run, choosing a direction towards his home less straight than he had at first intended; but hoping by his speed to get there before his dad arrived.

As the stiffness in his limbs wore off he went faster, hearing the thud of his steps on the hard pavement, and hearing, in spite of his efforts to shut it out, the mocking laughter, whispering faintly yet intimately to him alone, all the way as he went.

David stopped a moment on the steps before the front door, and heard his dad approaching at a slow pace from the other end of the street. He rushed into the house and was relieved to see Peter was there, sitting in a chair before the television, the dog at his feet. 'Everythin' O.K.? I got stuck at the library,'

David said breathlessly, in implausible and unnecessary excuse.

'Sure man. Ever'thin's O.K.,' Peter answered.

'I didn't expect to find you at home,' David said. 'Thought you'd be out with the boys.'

'No man. I gotta stay with her now she ready for have them puppies, you see,' Peter said. They both looked at the dog, and she sleepily raised her head and whimpered at Peter.

'Black is a gift.' David remembered the puzzling words. 'An' where's Lotty an' mum?' he asked to drive away the sound of that laughter, which had pursued him here and sounded again in his head.

'Lotty have gone to bed, an' mum gone to do some sewin' upstairs.'

Mrs Reynolds often did sewing for the people who lived on the floor above, as she did for many families in the area. It was a way to make a bit of extra money.

At this David heard his dad come into the house. He sat in a chair away from the television and opened one of his books. When his dad walked into the room he was able to give a good impression of having been home for some time. He was confident enough to say boldly: 'Hello dad, where you been?'

'Been askin' a man who know 'bout dogs how she goin' to make out,' his dad answered after some hesitation.

'An' what he say?' David continued.

'He say ever'thin' goin' to be jus' fine.' His dad answered more confidently this time, and then he went on: 'But never mind that, son, I axin' the questions here an' you answerin'! Where you think you been when you was wanted for lookin' after Lotty?'

'I been at the library tryin' to find how Allegro gonna make out too.'

'O, an' what you find?' his dad asked, diverted, interested in what the library had to say.

'Found that she goin' to be O.K., an' that brindled dogs like she is are likely to have black puppies.'

David looked closely at his father. He saw him half-smile and make a little nod to himself as he added two and two together. David knew the words that his father was pondering at this moment; they were: 'Black is a gift.'

CHAPTER THREE

Island in the Sun

DAVID was reading. It was all right in the living-room when there was only his mother there; but it grew more difficult the more the family gathered. Now, besides his mother, there was only Lotty, and so it was fairly quiet. Lotty was playing a game of her own that included a lot of low-pitched talking to herself and a good deal of affectionate chatter to the dog. Allegro was used to Lotty's fussiness now, and accepted it patiently. It was good preparation, Mrs Reynolds said, for when all those lively puppies came and were crawling all over her.

Mrs Reynolds counted on Allegro having a large litter, for her strict account of the cost of keeping the dog showed her that they would need to sell a fair number of puppies to make up their expenses. She grumbled aloud about these anxieties, and David, absorbed in his book, didn't let himself listen.

'That dog him more expensive to feed than a human bein', an' they're expensive enough,' she said.

'Am I expensive, mammy?' Lotty was always ready to talk, even if she didn't altogether understand what she was talking about.

'Here you are! In Jamaica we could keep the whole family on what it cost to keep you.'

Lotty liked to talk about Jamaica because everybody made it sound so lovely and exciting. 'Would

you be my teacher in Jamaica as well as my mammy?'
she asked.

'That is one of the few disadvantages, yes,' Mrs
Reynolds said, smiling at the private joke she shared
with David, for he glanced up from his book as she
answered. In Jamaica, in the village in St Catherine
where they had lived, Mrs Reynolds had been a
teacher of all subjects to all ages in the local school. In
England her qualifications weren't right; she had been
told she must do further teacher training before she
could be given work.

'An' tell me 'bout the sunshine,' Lotty said.

The sun burned white in the sky in all Mrs Reynolds's memories, and that made comparison with
England always weighted in favour of home. In the
sun you felt good, able to see things in the right
perspective; it made life simple. She looked now
at the children and the dog, all sitting close to the
paraffin stove, and she felt the cold that lay all around
this one room like a siege. How could she answer
Lotty? How could she describe a different world?

'Well child, we spends all our time, the whole year
round in the open air – outside, an' it warm everywhere. The air is fresh an' full of nice smells of plants
an' flowers growin'. Not like the smell of the old
stove!'

'You mean we lives an' has dinner outside – an'
sleeps?' Lotty was puzzled.

'Sometimes we has our meals out, yes; but we got a
house jus' the same as here, an' beds ...'

Mrs Reynolds went on to describe the house, how
it was made to suit the climate, and David, who

33

remembered it all, dwelt on the memories his mother had brought back of the white sun and the brightness of colour. He thought of the hills that were so far off that their colour melted into blue, but such a blue: more bright than any he had seen in England.

When she was asked to talk about Jamaica Mrs Reynolds didn't need much prompting, and she would often go on when she had answered the question, talking freely. David liked to hear her, because it gave him the chance to measure his memories against hers. He had been only six when they came to England, and he needed these reminders to keep it all clear.

'That's why it all cost cheaper,' his mother was saying, 'because we growed near ever'thin' we ate: sweet potato, yams, mangoes, bananas, plantains, watermelon, peas, beans – ever'thin'! An' they all use to ask my mother, your gran, where ever'thin' had to go, an' what to plant. An' she was boss of the whole thing, an' tell ever'body, uncles an' cousins, who all live with us on this land we got, what to do. An' when it come time for goin' to market she tol' what to take an' what to buy. An' 'course, when I growed an' learnt it all she say I must do it, because she couldn't get about so fast, an' her eyes wasn't so sharp. But o' course, they were; she watch ever'thin', even when she tell me to do it.

'Same with the sewin'. First she did it all for the whole family, then she say her eyes weren't no good for it any more an' I must do it. But she use to help an' do all the plain sewing when I had to be in school.'

David remembered how his mother had been the one who was at the centre of everything, not only in

their own family but in the whole of the little group of
houses that had made the village where all his
relations lived. And it was the same here in England.
That was why his dad had been afraid and in trouble
about the dog. It was why he was so anxious to know
about the puppies. He couldn't do anything as important as buying a one hundred pound greyhound
bitch without having his wife's approval for the plan;
for now, with her own contribution in dress-making,
child-minding, and as agent for various trading clubs,
she controlled the family finances; and if she seemed
stern it was because her task was hard, and her biggest
problem was with her husband, whose nature made it
difficult for him to grasp the desperate importance of
money in the changed way of life they led in this
country.

'But mammy, if the sun so warm an' everything,
why don't we go back to Jamaica an' live there?'
Lotty asked.

'We'll go back soon – one day – when that dog win
a thousand pound,' Mrs Reynolds answered idly. She
didn't know the answer to the question; Jamaica had
become a dream-country, and though she often wanted to be there, she had no intentions of going. She
thought as her husband thought – of being well-off
here; of having a proper house that was new and full
of the most modern fittings: central heating, an up-
to-date kitchen, bedrooms enough, and a real garden.
In England you couldn't think except in those terms,
because that was what life in England was all about,
and it wasn't easy to succeed. Certainly there was no
hope of succeeding if you let yourself dream about
sunshine and colour. You had to work at success,

and that was why she was trying to find time to fit in study, to enable her to qualify as a teacher and earn a better wage.

'Will Allegro ever win all that money, mammy?' Lotty asked, wide-eyed that such things could be.

'We'll be lucky if that dog don't cost us more than it win. I just hopes we gets our money back in the end, that's all, an' has lots of puppies with this pedigree that'll sell for twenty pounds each.'

'How many you think there'll be, mammy?'

'I dunno child, I hope five or six.'

'An' shall we be able to keep one if there are plenty – enough?'

'Oh no, for certain sure. We got nowhere to keep no puppy dog, an' what we want with racin' dogs, I wonder. Who goin' to tell me that?'

At this moment Mr Reynolds came home. He had been listening to advice from a friend, who told him that Allegro, being such a valuable dog, needed the services of a vet at this important time in her life. Without thought of the expense, Mr Reynolds made the suggestion at once:

'I been thinkin': to be on the safe side we needs to call in the vet when that dog reach her time.' He tried to imply that this must ensure a larger litter of puppies.

'Vet? Who you think goin' to pay for that?' Mrs Reynolds asked with scorn.

'Well, I reckon it goin' to be worth it in the end,' he added, a little set back by the directness and practicality of her question.

'We not havin' no vet here, 'ceptin' me, and Peter who know that dog like a brother. We never had no vet for animals before, an' I'm sure if I can manage three children without no doctorin' that dog goin' to manage havin' her puppies the same. So don' you go talkin' no more about it: payin' all that money we can't afford.'

'But it not the same,' he persisted, 'this dog have a pedigree ...'

'Oh, an' you think I got none?' she asked sharply, but she was teasing and not severe. 'I got as much pedigree as that dog have, an' she goin' to get no special care that you never did afford me.'

Mr Reynolds was relieved to be let off so lightly. He didn't offer any further defence of the idea; but he had meant no insult to his wife when he had talked about pedigree. He thought it meant being delicate in health, and his wife was certainly not that. He wondered if he could explain his meaning and decided he couldn't, so he went to switch on the television.

'Is there somethin' special you wants to see on there, because David is readin' an' it goin' to disturb him?' Mrs Reynolds said.

'It's O.K., mum, I can go to bed,' David said, getting up with his eyes still fixed on the page. He knew that his dad worked hard all day at the factory and that he was generally too tired to do much else but sit in the evening. He was a bit sorry too that his dad had got the worst of it again in argument; it wasn't that his mother was bossy, but she always said what she thought, and she thought more clearly than his dad.

He went straight through into the bedroom and was pleased that he'd been able to prevent another argument, especially as it made no difference to him so long as he could read. But, since he had begun to grow up and understand things, he had learnt that his mum and dad saw things in very different ways. His dad was easy-going and trusting; he had faith that things would work out. He was hopeful that the dog would earn them a lot of money, and he trusted the Obeahman's word that this would happen. His mum was of the opinion that things worked out only if you made them; she believed that the only way they could profit from the dog was by careful calculation: trying to balance present costs against future gains.

It was the same, though in a different way, with his reading: his dad wanted him to do well at school and later on in life; but it was only his mum who understood that if he was going to make a success of his learning he had to be given encouragement and opportunity now and all the time.

David did not remember how it had been in Jamaica, but he knew that here, in this country, being poor made the difference between his parents stand out more sharply, and especially now that they had the dog. This was an unusual and important matter of money on which they held very different views; he saw it clearly, but he tried not to be involved in their difference.

Now David heard the noise of the television; but it sounded distantly, and he settled under the glaring light of the naked bulb with his book half under the covers to read for as long as he could remain undisturbed. When Lotty came to bed there was a brief interruption, but she soon settled to sleep in her cot and he read on by the light of his torch under the bedclothes until the battery ran out.

He was still awake when Peter climbed in bed beside him, for after reading stopped he had played his favourite game of remembering all he could about the life in Jamaica. 'Where you been till this time?' he asked as Pete settled down beside him.

'Been out to the caff, man.' Peter always seemed to imply his own manhood when he called you 'man', as though he was reminding you how much older he was, and, in this case, how impertinent it was to ask him where he had been.

'What if Allegro had had her puppies while you were out?' David asked, knowing that it was a matter of pride with Peter that he was responsible for the dog.

'She not ready.'

'How you know, man?'

'I jus' know – I goin' to be there when it happen.'

'How do you know, Pete. We ever have a dog before – in Jamaica I mean?'

'Not like this, but I goin' to be there all the same. You see.'

CHAPTER FOUR

A Singular Event

DAVID did see, sooner than he expected. As usual next morning he walked sleepily into the living-room and was greeted by his mother: 'There's no wonder you tired. If you reads so late what you expect?'

David couldn't believe his eyes, for the first thing he saw was a tiny, spindly puppy, jet-black, blindly thrusting itself at Allegro's belly as she lay on her side in the box Peter had begged from the market for her. 'How many'd she have?' was David's first question.

'How many do you see?' his mother asked with a flatness in her voice that told him he saw in this one, frail, little creature all the puppies there were.

'Is that ... ?' he began, but daren't finish his question because he sensed the gloom around him. It *was* the only one, and David went down on his knees before Allegro and the puppy as much to escape the embarrassment of his uncompleted question as to look closely at this tiny black dog, which was like a consolation prize for the disappointment of their high hopes. 'Black is a gift,' David thought. The words might fit, but how cruelly small and single the gift had turned out to be. And the other promise that his dad would have as many puppies as he needed, what about that? It just showed, he thought, how foolish it was to listen to the nonsense that Obeahmen talked. How could this one, pathetic, little creature repay his father for all he had spent?

David looked up now at his dad, who sat dejectedly in his chair staring at the carpet with nothing to say for himself. Peter was sitting close to the dogs, and, after a quick glance at his mum's face, David decided that his brother was the only one who was approachable at this time. 'Are there goin' to be any more?' he asked him, guarding the question from his parents by using the quietest tone.

'No, there only one. She not havin' any more.'

'How do you know?' David asked with some challenge; it seemed unusual for a dog to have only one puppy.

'Because I have been with her since three o'clock 's mornin'. It all happen hours ago, an' she got it all over an' done with.'

David found it too difficult to argue any further with his brother, who had obviously sat up all night with Allegro while he had lain cosy and warm asleep. Sadly, he accepted the unpleasant truth, as the rest of them had done earlier, and adopted a suitable air of glumness, while the puppy, unaware of the disappointment he was to them all, unaware even of their existence, thrust himself with skinny, wriggling body and gawky, scrambling legs upon his mother, seeking his food.

David looked closely at the tiny, black paws on which every nail was perfect. How brand-new they all were, how unused! He thought of the pedigree that would show these paws, and wondered how it would distinguish this from other dogs. Wouldn't it be just the same?

His thoughts were interrupted by the sudden appearance of his sister from the bedroom. She was always the last of the family to appear in the morning, but she came none the less lively for that.

'Oh, the puppies have come!' she cried with delight, and in a trance of love, ready-made for the moment, she rushed towards the box with her hands stretched eagerly to take up and hug the one tiny black baby she could see. She wanted to hold it close and pour out in a torrent her words of love and her kisses.

But she didn't get near enough to touch. As soon as he saw her intent Peter leapt from his chair and caught her. She it was who was snatched up and held close, a captive in Peter's arms. He sat down again in his chair, holding Lotty on his knees; and, as she struggled, not understanding, and impatient still to snatch the puppy, he explained to her in gentle words yet firm that the puppy was too small to touch and was certainly not to be hugged and kissed.

'I want him, he lovely,' she persisted.

'He very weak an' no one even gotta touch him yet. If you tries to take him out o' that box Allegro goin' to be so scared you tryin' to hurt him that she gonna take a snap at you. So don' you touch.'

When she was freed, Lotty had to content herself with standing at a distance, murmuring her words of love, and giggling at the puppy's comic antics as it continued its single-minded efforts to feed. Lotty laughed out loud when it rolled over and fell off. She watched it pick itself up and start to climb again; but the puppy paid no more heed to her attentions than it did to the rest of the family, who went glumly about their preparations for the day.

David feared that the gloom that had stood over the

household at breakfast time was going to last; and he dreaded the atmosphere he would find when he came home from school in the afternoon. He was surprised to detect no sign of it; his mother was cheerful with Lotty and seemed to be in her best humour when she greeted him. It was typical of him to go cautiously with people, and he watched her for some time just to make sure that he hadn't been mistaken; he didn't want to go and say anything stupid that would upset or rouse her. But he needn't have worried; she had obviously decided to make the best of it, and she had no doubt worked out a plan that was practical, that would cut their losses. She was certainly not in one of her rare anxiety moods about money, and her first words showed she had accepted the situation: 'That puppy dog kep' your brother in this house all day long. I had to send him out in the end to get some air.'

'Why, what he been doin'?' David asked.

'Doin'? He been doin' nothin'. Jus' sittin' there strokin' Allegro an' watchin' that puppy dog.'

'I didn't know he was so fond of dogs.'

'Always was fond. An' he seem to know no end about trainin' greyhounds. He tell me beside them books you read he been talkin' outside all he can to a man he know who has kept racin' dogs. I do declare Peter is all ready to start trainin' that puppy 'most as soon as he can walk.'

'It said in the book that you can't start too early trainin' them to go for the lure,' David remembered and said.

' "Lure"? What's the lure?' his mother asked.

'Why, anything that attracts the dog – a bit of fur, or a stuffed toy – you drag it in front of him and egg

43

him on to try and catch it. If they'll do that it mean they'll follow the hare on the race-track.'

'The hare? You don' mean to tell me he goin' to train that puppy dog to kill?'

'No mum, the hare's not a real one, it's just like a stuffed toy; but it's fastened on a rail round the race-track an' driven in front of the dogs to make them run. They never even catch it 'cos it can always be driven faster than they can run.'

His confidence in his mum's amiability was restored by her attentiveness to his explanation, and David went on to ask: 'You goin' to let him keep that puppy an' train it to race, mum?'

His mother laughed, prepared herself to make a long answer about how foolish it was to think you could profit by gambling on dog-racing, and then suddenly decided she didn't want to give a lecture and said: 'No, when that puppy is old enough to leave its mother we goin' to sell both of them an' hope to get back as much as we can of what we lost. That's why I been tellin' Lotty here she mustn't get too fond of them.'

David was shocked by the calm statement of her plan. He knew it was the only sensible thing to do; but after she had accepted the dog, Allegro, into the house, how could she now talk so easily about selling both puppy and mother as well? Though David had not had many dealings with Allegro, because of her condition and because of the dark, cold winter nights that had kept them all inside, he had imagined that Allegro was part of his life now, and a member of the family.

But whatever his mother said at this time there were many weeks to go before the puppy would be ready to sell. And, though his mum had told Lotty not to grow too fond of it, who knew what would happen during those weeks? Perhaps she herself would weaken and find that she couldn't part with the puppy at the end of that time. Anything could happen.

And indeed, as the weeks went slowly by, the puppy did become part of the family. He grew stronger and he grew more lively; and though he was confined to the house all the time, he lost no opportunity to run and leap and turn; he was always active. From the first attempt that Peter made to attract him with the lure – one of Lotty's old stuffed rabbits on a string – he sprang and bounded after it whenever he was tempted. Sometimes David would play the game with him, and David liked to turn about on the spot, dangling the lure and sweeping it round in a circle just above the ground as fast as he could. Then the puppy would run untiringly round after it, rapidly overcoming his ungainliness, and learning to thrust himself always into the constant turn with his outside legs, until he acquired such agility and speed that David could not guard the lure for long from the snap of his sharp, puppy bite.

They called him Jet. That was David's name, and everybody agreed that it was apt, because the puppy's entire coat was polished black like jet-stone – even his eyes sparkled black. And in his movements he was so silent and fleet that it seemed as if he was powered by electricity. Besides its lustre, David told the family, jet generates static electricity. That was why you could rub it and things were attracted to it. 'And', David went on in triumph to justify further his choice of name, 'when he runs he goes like a jet.'

But sometimes, when the room was rather sombre – perhaps just before the lights went on in the evening – David would look at Jet as he lay still, asleep, or toying idly with his mother's tail, and he would see the lustre gone from the puppy's coat and the light in his eye dimmed. The coat then seemed as black as soot, so dense a black that it suggested empty space to David's mind. 'Shadow,' David thought then, for he liked to consider other names; their sounds and their meanings gave him pleasure. But 'Shadow' depended on something solid: Jet was real enough in himself, even if he did have that air as he moved of being outside the laws of gravity.

Next David thought of 'Pluto', King of the Underworld. The name suited because it suggested the darkness and the mystery he saw in the young dog; but he thought of Walt Disney's Pluto and he knew the name was no good; there was nothing comic about this dog. This was Pluto, the King, the God.

Soon winter gave place to spring. The evenings lengthened, but the rains of February and March made the ground heavy, and the long stretches of grass in the park where Peter and his dad and sometimes David took the dogs to give them exercise were not yet right for real training, though Allegro and Jet enjoyed being allowed to run.

Now that it was warmer they were moved outside, back into the play-house which Lotty was persuaded to give up to them in exchange for an indoor one that her dad and Peter patiently built for her in the bedroom.

The whole back yard was given over to the dogs,

and, though it wasn't smart with wire fence and cedar-wood shed to house them, the decayed brick walls served as well, and the size of the yard was adequate for the dogs to stretch their legs at play.

Mrs Reynolds, true to David's prediction, didn't hurry on the sale of either dog; but her readiness to wait after the three months when the puppy was weaned was not due simply to her becoming fond of Jet, as David had supposed. She had soon realized the need to understand something about racing dogs, and she too had gone to the library and sought books on the subject. A conversation between his parents when Jet was nearing three months old had surprised David, for they seemed to have changed positions on the subject. His dad had had enough, and was anxious to be rid of the dogs, while his mother found reasons for keeping them. 'I think it time for them to go outside back into that shed,' she had said at first.

'I think it time for them to go be sold,' he answered, hoping his show of readiness would please her.

'No, I think you wrong. It too soon.'

'But I been talkin' to some fellahs, an' they say I goin' to get easy twenty-five pound for that puppy, an' perhaps even fifty pound if I lucky. An' Allegro'll fetch more 'n another fifty, so we goin' to get back all that money they cost.'

'But you forgettin' they costs three pounds a week to keep all this time. Where you goin' to get that back? No, man, we gotta keep that puppy for a year, bring him up like a racin' dog with lots of exercise, an' then take him to the racin'-track an' give him a trial. Then we goin' to see what sort of a dog he turn out. He might be worth hundreds of pounds if he can make a good time at that trial.'

'But what about Allegro, you think she gotta go?'

'No, man, she has to stay, make company for the puppy. But no reason why she shouldn't go do some racin' now, an' we'll see how she make out.'

'But they has to go to a trainer at the dog-track and stay there if they wants to race.'

'No, they can be trained at home. They has to spend twenty-four hours at the track before a race, that's all. It goin' to be cheaper for us to keep them, an' Peter got plenty time to spend on them. They just wants some gear for the trainin'; but I reckon I got a husband who can manage that if he haven't forgotten how to use hammer and nails.'

Mr Reynolds smiled happily. He liked to be set to work with his carpenter's tools. In Jamaica he had been a joiner; but he too had found work at his trade difficult to get in this country. 'I ready to build a greyhound stadium if that's what you wants,' he said.

CHAPTER FIVE

Jet Makes a Special Impression

THE first job Mr Reynolds was set to do was to build the play-house to replace the one Lotty had given up in the coal-shed. She was happy with the exchange, and the dogs were housed in conditions more suited to dogs in training; for keeping them in the house made them soft and spoiled them for hard work.

Next, on his wife's instructions, and after a visit to the dog-track, Mr Reynolds designed and made a trap that was set up in the yard, but that was collapsible and light enough to carry out to the park when the dogs went there for exercise.

'Why do they need that, mammy?' Lotty asked.

'They got to learn to accept bein' put in there before the race start, and they has to learn to come shootin' out when the hare goes past an' the door is opened for them.'

But the trap was no good without a hare. It was all right in the yard where Peter could work the lure, dragging it quickly past the trap for David to release the dog from inside to spring and run and pounce. But the problem was to keep him running, and this was where Mr Reynolds's best piece of gadgetry came in. Again, he had to work from advice, but once he had been told the principle of the machinery they needed, the rest was easy. Peter went round the

scrap-yards and bought an old bicycle frame with pedals and chain still good. Mr Reynolds attached a drum-like cylinder to the rear cog, and made the frame to stand stable when turned upside-down, with steel struts for legs in place of the seat and the handlebars. Now, when the pedals were turned like a handle, the drum turned. A length of strong string with the stuffed rabbit at the end of it was fastened to the drum, so that when the pedals turned at speed the string would wind round the drum and, as it reeled in, it pulled the lure along fast enough to give the dogs a run.

A last piece of necessary equipment was a muzzle for the puppy. When dogs went on the track they had to wear muzzles because any bickering and snapping among them could obviously spoil the race. Mr Reynolds bought a muzzle, and with patient effort they persuaded Jet to accept it as regular wear when he ran.

David went along with Peter and his dad to help at the first trial they held in the park. It needed one person to work the machine, and it was easier when two started the dogs. Peter worked the machine, David put Allegro into the trap, and his dad held Jet alongside. As the hare flashed by, David sprang the trap, and Mr Reynolds let Jet slip, all in a moment.

Allegro knew what to do; she shot from the trap and went hurtling, low to the ground, with kicking heels. Her body seemed to fold and stretch with a tremendous thrust from her back legs; and, with each rapid, wavy repetition of the movement, she kicked up tufts of grass and soft earth behind her all the way. In direct line she sped after the bobbing hare, until, at the end of its course, she overran it as the machine slowed. Then she turned, arcing back towards Peter, to be patted for her efforts.

Jet did not show any of his mother's urgency that first time; he was unfamiliar with this routine and went bounding off gamely, yet playfully, in pursuit of Allegro. It was only when he realized that this was serious running that he laid his ears back and tracked her from behind. He was too young and too small yet to match her speed, but it gave David a queer, excited feeling to see this young, black dog running all-out for the first time. How strange it was that he had such an instinct for running, and was gifted with the perfect action, untaught and unpractised.

'Gifted' – David thought again of the word he had

used, and felt an odd sense that Jet was unusual. He knew nothing about racing-dogs; but there was such fluency in this puppy's movement, and such an air of assurance about him – he looked perfect, unflawed from the black tip of his nose to the black tip of his tail – that David knew he must be special.

Next time they ran the same thing happened; Jet ran in pursuit of his mother and was not apparently aware that the real aim was to run down the hare. 'Try him in the trap,' David suggested to his dad.

It was the same again, though this time Jet was slower to start.

'He not goin' after the hare, is he?' Mr Reynolds said.

'No, Allegro's too fast off the mark so he think he chasin' her.'

'This time we goin' to let him go first, then he goin' to chase the hare an' think Allegro chasin' him,' Mr Reynolds decided. To do this they put Allegro in the trap and arranged that David should wait until Jet was away in pursuit of the hare before he released her.

The hare went bumping over the ground, the string snaking through the grass before it, and Mr Reynolds held Jet close to the path of the hare so that he would be sure to see it as it flopped by. Sure enough, Jet threw his weight after it as it bounced past him, and Mr Reynolds let him go at once. With his eye on this strange creature that went at such challenging speed, Jet went off like an arrow, and ran faster than he had done ever before to try to catch it. David was amazed when he had released Allegro to see the little dog holding his own, running for all he was worth and giving ground to Allegro only on the second half of the course.

And so they let the puppy run, and, at the end of the session, Mr Reynolds and both the boys were as flushed with their success in arranging it so professionally as the dogs were from their exercise. David did not say anything yet to the others of his feelings about Jet, but he watched both his father and Pete to see whether there was anything in their attitudes to the puppy that would tell him their feelings.

It was in Pete that he noticed something. His brother's expression as he regarded Jet bore the same look of wonder as David felt himself, and he saw that he wasn't alone in being impressed. But he decided that it was too soon to speak; Pete liked to be matter-of-fact, and would probably deny that there was anything to make a fuss about; and so David contented himself with the knowledge of Pete's special interest, and he decided that if he spoke at all now it should be to his mother. Mrs Reynolds had played a major role in organizing the dogs' training, but she took no active part in it, and hadn't seen Jet run; it was only right, therefore, that David should give her his impressions of their progress.

When they came home and had put the dogs in the yard, Pete, whose regular job it was, came into the kitchen to prepare their food.

'I want to give them their dinner,' Lotty said with a note of complaint in her voice, for she had not accepted the loss of the dogs, and especially Jet, as toys which she could hug and kiss like her dolls. At seven it is difficult to imagine that dogs can have any other use.

'Very well, you come with me,' Pete said as he picked up what dishes he could carry, 'you take Jet's food an' carry it careful.'

So, proudly, yet having only half her own way, for feeding the dogs was not as exciting as playing with them, Lotty followed Pete outside. David followed the two of them because something in Lotty's eagerness caught his notice.

When the food was set down Pete went back into the house and Lotty, seeing her opportunity, went down beside the puppy as he ate, first to stroke him, and then, as she felt the stronger desire, to smother him with her love. David did not interfere because he felt the same urge in himself, though of course he was too grown-up to give way to it.

But there was no need to be anxious for the dog; it was almost as if he stiffened at Lotty's touch, and drew himself up tense. David saw the lustre of his coat appear in fluid motion as the light slid over the sudden electric disturbance of the hair. He raised his head from the dish and turned it a fraction away from her in a gesture that seemed to express discouragement; and then, when Lotty persisted, he moved bodily and took up another position on the opposite side of his dish, out of her reach.

'He want to eat his dinner, Lotty,' David said, mildly, 'he've been workin' very hard an' be very hungry.'

Suspiciously Lotty asked, 'What have he been doin'?' for she had no ideas about dogs working at all. But David explained patiently how much running Jet had done, 'And it given him ever such a big appetite.'

She stood away, and yet she waited to pounce once

more when Jet was finished, and it looked as though that might be shortly. But Peter returned before Lotty had a chance to approach a second time; and now, though Jet was more friendly, she had to be content to pat and stroke him as he came to her and invited it; he would not be held.

David felt an understanding of this; Jet disliked being touched because he was sensitive, he was all energy, and the touching broke into his completeness and stole from it.

When he was alone with his mother David said, 'What you want to keep that puppy for, mum?'

She looked at him sharply, finding his question strange. 'I tol' you why, because he goin' to fetch a better price when he be a bit older – old enough to race.'

'But what if he don' run well enough?' David wanted his mother to give an opinion of the puppy; he knew her well enough to guess that she had already made a shrewd judgement of Jet from the dog's appearance alone.

'I think he goin' to run all right. I never see a dog better made for it. Runnin's all he goin' to be good for ever, if you asks me.'

'What make you say that when you haven't seen him?' David asked.

'I dunno. There's no need to see him. I just knows he can do it. I got that feelin'.'

And David was satisfied. His mother had noticed the same thing about Jet, and what was important was that it was not just wishing for the dog to succeed; it was different from his dad's reliance on Obeah. His mother had looked at the dog and seen something that was firm evidence of its speed. She couldn't define what it was any more than he could himself. She couldn't describe it, and no more could he. He could only say that it was some energy inside the dog like electricity that was so obvious in him even at rest that it made him special – different from other greyhounds.

It didn't matter somehow that there was only the serene temperament of his mother, Allegro, to compare him with. David was sure he would recognize that specialness anyway. It was like when he had started at the Comprehensive and they had gone out for football. In the other form that shared their games period David had seen one boy, small, and you would have thought insignificant, who had marks left by his glasses over the bridge of his nose. Yet just from the way he looked in his football strip David had told himself, 'I bet he's the best player.' Within five minutes of the kick-off David heard the P.E. teacher asking the kid's name, and before they had played much longer, this boy, Scattergood, was commanding his team and making everyone else look silly.

If it was the same with Jet, it was important that they should keep him; he might win them the thousand pounds that could take them back to Jamaica. David didn't say anything to Pete or to his dad yet; though he was interested to know their opinions, he was shy, and didn't want them to think him foolish. They might fail to see or to heed what he saw in the dog. Anyway, Peter was likely to have too favourable a view of Jet, and so was his dad; both of them had more at stake on the puppy, and both of them would be bound to defend him.

But, though he was trying to be unbiased, David

found it very difficult to stop thinking about one thousand pound prizes. When you had a little bit of ground to base your hope upon, it was surprising what a lofty tower of exciting prospects you could raise from that ground.

At night he asked Peter if he could go to shut the dogs in. Peter didn't begrudge him so unimportant a job, and he went out alone into the backyard, holding his torch unlit in his hand. Allegro came up to him and rubbed her head against him. He patted her, and stroked her absently, looking for the other. In the dark there was no sign.

David scanned the yard, looking for movement. He thought how Jet was one now with this darkness, how his blackness had melted into it, so that he had no visible body, but was just a force, a spirit in the night. The thought made him shudder, and he clicked on the torch and swung the beam at dog-height round the yard. Suddenly the beam showed two red spots that glowed like fire-coals. 'Jet,' he called, still hesitant, 'come boy!'

David clicked off his torch, and he felt rather than saw Jet's movement towards him; it was like a disturbance of the air, a wind. But Jet bounded around him now, and David felt his strength as he and Allegro were buffeted by the puppy who, now he had come into the narrow space by the kennel, chose to be frolicsome. 'In you go,' David said, giving Jet a hopeful push inside after his mother. Jet bounded in, but he would have been out again as quick had not David closed the door and secured the hasp and padlock quickly upon him.

'Jet Black.' He thought of a name. But the two

words meant the same thing. 'Jet Stone.' No, for 'Stone' gave a wrong idea of heaviness. 'Jet Stream', then. As he walked into the house David considered the merits of this addition to the name.

CHAPTER SIX

At the Races

ALL through the summer the regular sessions of training continued. Allegro went back to racing and was graded on her return to the track so that she could enter races where she had an even chance of doing well. Sometimes she won, and, though the stakes were never high, her modest success was enough to show a little gain. The cost of paying for her by monthly instalments and the cost of feeding both dogs was not entirely dead-loss.

The whole family had to go, of course, to see her first race; and this was a very special event, particularly for David, to whom a racing stadium was a place of mystery.

The track was not in the best part of town, but then neither was the place where they lived. And, like their home, the track was a complete little world of its own: an oval, as shut off from the busy, grimy town outside as was Wembley Stadium. Anyway, they saw little of the town on the way there, for the night was dark, and the only suggestion of the character of the area was given by poor street lighting and the flash of car headlights. It wasn't until they came to the stadium car-park, and the lights were so bright that they dazzled, that David really became aware of the surrounding drabness.

But Mr Reynolds hadn't come to view the town; he ushered them through the turnstiles, where, when they

were all assembled, they were met by a man who gave
them their race-cards. Importantly, the children walked behind their parents carrying these cards. 'I
wonder if they can tell we are owners?' David asked
himself, proudly, as he looked into the faces that
were white and seemingly surprised in the strange,
bright light. 'Do you know that Allegro in the third
race is our dog?' he wanted to say to them.

Slowly the Reynolds walked round the track towards the enclosure and the kennels. The track itself
was bright green beneath the continuous row of
brilliant floodlights that lined the inside wall on
standards ten yards apart. David saw the hare at rest
at the end of a long metal arm that was swung out
over the track, and on the outer rail he noticed the
electric fittings that drove the hare round. 'The same
idea as the drive on dodgem cars,' he thought.

The enclosed space in the centre of the stadium was
a patch of dark night, for none of the lights was
directed into it. 'Obeahland,' David told himself. But
strangely, in spite of the blackness of that space, beyond it you could see the other side of the stadium no
less bright than where they were. The night sky above
seemed a black dome, starless and impenetrable,
which roofed over the stadium and cut them off from
the world.

They passed before the grandstand, which was
covered and rose in steep steps to give a view of the
whole track. By the rail in front of it stood the bookmakers with their little tables and their blackboards,
ready to take bets. There was a smaller stand far over
to the other side of the stadium, and the bookmakers
had men in the grandstand on the steps above them

to signal information to their assistants on the other side. When his dad pointed these men out to him David was a bit puzzled to imagine it, but his dad said, 'You wait till the bettin' start an' look for them, they wears white gloves to be seen clear; they called tick-tack men.'

Now they came to the kennels with a high wired fence round them. There was a group of dogs wearing their race-coats walking up and down the yard on the other side of the wire. Each dog was on a lead held by a kennel-maid, and they were having their muzzles put on before being led out to walk round the track to the traps.

Mr Reynolds looked carefully through the fence at the dogs and began to study his race-card. 'I think I decided what I fancy for the first race,' he said, 'so I goin' to tell 'bout the race-card an' we see if any of you can come up with a winner.' He explained the complicated information that was given in abbreviations on the card, and told them to try to judge the dogs from this and pick the likely winner of the race that was coming up. 'You takes the size an' character an' how they run in their last races into account when you decides,' he said.

When they had all thought carefully, he said, 'Well now, what's it to be, Lotty?'

'Little Lulu,' she said, straight out.

'Why that?' he asked.

'It the name I like best,' she answered, 'an' look, it a lovely fawn colour.'

'Well, a lot of money been made choosin' winners that way. What you fancy, Barbara?' he asked his wife.

'Well I like two, I can't make up me mind. Apache Arrow has won two of its last races, but they were the first two of the five an' it have always started badly. Will o' the Wisp won his last race, an' he a big strong dog. I think I choose him.'

'Very good. Will o' the Wisp. Now David.'

'Oliver Twist,' David said, and he didn't need to explain why he had chosen the dog with the name of a favourite book. The rest of them laughed.

'Now Peter?' Mr Reynolds asked.

'I think Will o' the Wisp.'

'Good,' said his dad. 'Now I tell you what I goin' to put my money on. My choice is Will o' the Wisp. So, I goin' to put ten pence on him for each of us that chose him, an' the same with the other races: the dog that gets most votes goin' to be the one I backs. If we all chooses the same dog that make fifty pence I put on him, O.K.?'

Everybody agreed, and the dogs came out now to walk round the track. Mr Reynolds led the children to the tote. They weren't going to place any bets, of course, even Peter was too young for that. David asked his dad what 'tote' meant.

'It a machine that count the money bet on each dog in the race, then fixes the share of the takings that goin' to be paid out to the winners. The less money been put on a dog, the more you gets back for each ten pence you betted on him.'

'How that different from the bookmakers then?' David asked.

'Ah, it different 'cos the bookmakers fixes their odds before the race; the tote work them out after.'

David thought he understood. 'If I put ten pence on

at 5 to 1 with a bookie I get fifty pence plus my stake money back – sixty pence. If I put ten pence on the same dog on the tote it depends how many others have backed him an' what share of the total money have been betted on that dog. I might get 6 to 1 if only a few have fancied him; I might get 2 to 1 if a lot of money goes on him.'

'That's right,' his dad said, 'you got the idea.'

Mr Reynolds placed his bet and they all returned to the rail to watch the dogs walk round the track and to be ready for the race. It was a fair distance all the way round, and the kennel-maids walked slowly in line. David thought they looked like those cutouts you make by folding paper into concertina folds. When you cut and unfold it the figures are all in line, holding hands. This cut-out was very much more skilful than David could have done: the dogs were so slender, their legs moved gracefully and were clearly defined, black against the light beyond them on the far side of the track. He could see the leads, stretching taut, or drooping slack, as the dogs pulled eagerly or loitered. Even the fine, curved lines of the muzzles were clear to be seen.

And so they went, slowly, stopping sometimes to face the grandstand and let the spectators take note of them. As they passed the Reynoldses the whole family looked eagerly at Will o' the Wisp, and were pleased to see how big and loping he was.

'Look now at those men in the stand – see their white gloves like I said,' Mr Reynolds urged them to look where he pointed. David easily picked out the men and was fascinated by their strange antics. They stood with one eye on the bookmakers' boards below them at the foot of the stand; with the other they looked across the stadium to their friends. And they were all busy waving their arms, giving information about the betting – for the odds were constantly changing – in a complicated sign language. David watched one of them holding his arms above his head and rapidly twirling his hands around each other. All these men kept busy and warm, no doubt, until the dogs entered the traps, and the chalked figures beside their names on the bookmakers' boards were worked out to their final form.

'Now for it,' Mr Reynolds said.

A silence fell over the whole stadium as the dogs were put in the traps. They were familiar with the whole procedure, and didn't offer any resistance even at this very delicate stage of the evening.

David felt his excitement mounting and had to turn away a moment to try to relieve his tension. He noticed the great, gaily painted results board that was designed in comic patterns like those toy computers they had on children's T.V. programmes, all decorated in the colours of the fairground. But the board didn't hold his attention; he was arrested again by the silence that was almost painful.

Suddenly, with a shock, a sound like humming started, and it seemed to come from every part of the stadium, as if everything were vibrating and threatening to shake into pieces. It took some moments to realize what was happening, but the movement of the hare around the other side of the track was so appropriate to the sound that David understood and was held spellbound by the speed of it.

'Swoosh!' The hare curved around the bend and

came rocketing towards them up the straight. Its ears were swept back and it gave little, regular, up and down motions of its body as it sped by. But before it was past there was the sharp report of the traps opening, and David's eyes were drawn away to see six dogs burst out and streak towards them all in a bunch.

With necks stretched they thrust their heads eagerly forward, and their bodies rocked evenly in the urgency

of their speed. Tails straight out behind, they folded and unfolded their legs in tremendous elastic stretches. Little Lulu was just in front.

'Will o' the Wisp!' Mr Reynolds shouted as they saw the greybrindled haunches of the dog turning the bend well up with the leaders; his heels kicked up turf, he was going strong.

Now the dogs were entering the far straight, stringing out at this view, and Little Lulu had lost the lead. Oliver Twist wasn't in it, he had gone wide and glanced the rail at the bend, losing his stride. It wasn't yet clear which dog led, for the first three had bunched. Now they rounded the second bend. 'Will o' the Wisp is there! Watch him finish!' Mr Reynolds shouted with excitement. And Will o' the Wisp began to pull away, out in front until he was two lengths clear. As he came up to them the second time David saw what looked like a smile of triumph on his face. But that did not hold him back; he went under the lights of the finish like a bullet, and on round the bend once more, his speed slowly relaxing till he came to his handler round the other side and stopped. Now he wagged his tail and was fussed by the kennel-maid for his splendid win.

Mr Reynolds smiled broadly; he had won too, it didn't matter how much. 'How about that dog?' he asked.

'Huh! Oliver Twist would have won easy if he hadn't hit the side,' David said.

'And Little Lulu was winnin',' Lotty cried, anxious to give her dog credit for the short spell of glory she'd enjoyed.

'Never mind, you have more chances,' Mr Reynolds

66

told them, 'you only gotta look more close at the dogs in the next race – see if you can find the winner this time.'

So they fell to studying their race-cards, and Peter had half an eye on his dad because they had to go and collect their winnings. Any money he had helped to win was important; it made up a little for his having no wages. Perhaps now he had won fifty pence for his dad, and if he took the same care in choosing his fancy for the second race he might be successful again.

When they went to the tote Mr Reynolds said, 'I don' think we shall have made our fortunes, but it better 'n losin'.'

He came back and showed his winnings; it was one pound eighty. 'Not so bad, eh?' he laughed.

Peter ran back to them and and said excitedly, 'It pay 5 to 1,' and he explained to David that five times thirty made one pound and fifty pence, plus their stake money, that made one-eighty. David was as excited and pleased as if he had picked the winner too. It seemed so easy.

The next race was coming up, and they had to give their attention to the important job of choosing again. They did it with care. This time David picked the same dog as his dad: Star Trek. It came in last and their twenty pence was lost. That proved it wasn't so easy, and David was a bit shocked.

Allegro was running in the next race, so, of course, nobody bothered to study the form of the other dogs; they just chose Allegro automatically.

'Swoosh!' went the hare and came sweeping towards them. The traps opened and again six dogs bounded. But Allegro had started badly, she seemed boxed-in behind. They saw her slanting out to the rails as she came up towards them and, as she passed, she had just found clear-way on the outside. But she was still trailing, and on the outside rail she had further to run when they came to the bend. In a flurry the six dogs went into the turn, their breath panting. The children shouted long for Allegro though they could see nothing of the placings in the shifting angles of the bend.

But their faith seemed to have worked, for, when the dogs rounded into the straight, Allegro was still there, hanging on grimly.

'She'll do it!' Mr Reynolds shouted, his eyes fixed on the dog, and a grin gradually spreading over his face. David had to look away, for he couldn't bear the tension of watching for Allegro to close the gap. Down the back straight inch by inch she did it, and before the last bend she was placed to cut across to the inner rail. But there was something in her that wouldn't let her take that advantage, she was going to run in wide.

'Cut in! Cut in!' Mr Reynolds shouted, but what was the use of that? Allegro wasn't interested in advice. Perhaps she was thinking: 'I've done all the hard work on the outside, that's where I'll stay.' She took the bend wide, but, astonishingly, she came into the last straight a good length in front, and went shooting past them so near that they could almost have stretched out hands to touch her.

'Well! What you think about that?' Mr Reynolds said, amazed and delighted. 'I never see a dog run a race like that. She must have done it just to show off because we all here to see her.'

This time the wait for him to come with the

winnings was an excitement shared by everybody; but when he came and showed them the takings in pound notes it was like a dream. The sight of his tight-held clutch of notes struck them dumb.

CHAPTER SEVEN

Beating the Clock

MR REYNOLDS's delight when Allegro won was un-affected by the thought that he was merely pulling back a little on his expenses. He didn't have enough respect for money to bother too much about balancing his books; but Mrs Reynolds, while sharing in his pleasure if Allegro won forty pounds, must always go back to her figures, and work out how many instal-ments that money would pay, or how much feed it would provide. She knew that Allegro's successes didn't happen often enough to put them in profit. After one such win she was able to say: 'That put us just level; but we got a money order to send this week.'

And so Allegro did her best on the track and was companion and rival in training to Jet. As the puppy grew bigger and stronger, he caught up in perfor-mance with his mother, and could run with her, neck and neck, in pursuit of the hare that was still the old, stuffed toy that Lotty had discarded. After so many rapid and bumpy journeys across the park it was much the worse for wear; it had lost an ear, and spilled out stuffing from one of its seams.

'I borrowed a stop-watch,' said Mr Reynolds one week-end. 'I thought we better see what that puppy can do. He goin' to be ready for his trial before long.'

Peter looked at David and winked. It would be four months yet before Jet was a year old; his speed now could tell them very little. But they gave way to their

father's impatience and went along to the park, interested themselves to play with the stop-watch and to see what time Jet would take to run the measured distance.

Peter was cleverest at controlling the hare, and he liked to be there to receive the dogs and fuss them when they had run. So it was between David and his father to decide who was to have the clock. 'You better work it,' Mr Reynolds said, 'I want to watch him run.' He was not very confident of his own speed of reaction, so David took the stop-watch and stood opposite Peter and the machine at the end of the run, ready to start the clock as soon as he saw the trap open.

Mr Reynolds had some difficulty in holding one dog and putting the other, Jet, into the trap; and, as he waited, David realized that he hadn't often watched the running from this end of the course; he would be able to see the dogs coming head-on towards him.

Mr Reynolds gave the signal and then he released the dogs. Whether it was the strangeness of being at this end David didn't know, but the dogs seemed to grow visibly bigger, so fast was their approach. They came with a smooth motion that was silent without effort, for there was no more than a snaky up and down rise and fall of the head, as though the dogs' speed was achieved by a rocker-mechanism inside them that gave them thrust. There was no more than a length between them as they came past the machine. Allegro's greater strength had enabled her to pull back the advantage Jet's early burst had given him. David stopped the clock precisely, and walked over to Peter.

The dogs had wheeled round and come in panting, tongues lolling. Peter and David patted them in turn as, restlessly, they moved about from one to the other of the boys.

'How'd he do?' Peter asked.

'Oh, not bad,' David answered coolly, showing the clock.

Peter made a quick calculation, scratched his head, and looked hard at David in silence. David returned his look. Peter was about to speak, but then he changed his mind, and turned to look at the dog, which had gone back running to meet their father.

'Did he do well?' Mr Reynolds asked, coming up.

'Not so badly,' said Peter in a matter-of-fact voice.

'He did a fantastic run for his age, but Pete thinks I stopped the watch too soon,' said David.

Pete laughed. 'Yeah, a good second too soon,' he said.

'No, he couldn't be as eager as me,' said Mr Reynolds.

'I was a bit late really because he had reached the line before I let myself react. You should start switchin' off jus' before he reach the line for to get the exact time,' David argued.

'I dunno 'bout that,' Pete said, 'but come on, let's have another go, you take the machine,' he said to David, 'I take the watch.'

'You don' distrust me, do you?' David said, pretending to be insulted, but Peter was fixing the strings under the dogs' collars for his dad to take them down to the start again, and pretended not to hear. David went to the machine, making the hare ready for his dad to draw out down to the start.

Mr Reynolds walked the two dogs and set the hare
at the length of its line some distance beyond the trap.
Then he put Jet into the trap, held Allegro ready on
the slip-string, and gave David the signal to start.

You had to start the pedals slowly, and smoothly
pick up pace, so that when the hare was passing the
trap it went already at top speed. It was his dad's job
to bother about slipping the dogs; David knew he had
to concentrate on that rapid build-up of speed: faster
than the dogs, but not so fast as to leave them far
behind, or endanger the machine.

It demanded all his concentration, and he worked
as hard this time as the dogs. But he controlled the
hare smoothly, and soon the dogs were past him and
turning shortly to come to him for their congratula-
tions. As he patted them he looked to Peter to learn
what time he had recorded. 'Well?' he called. 'Any
different?'

'Not really, more or less the same,' Pete answered,
looking a bit sheepish. He showed the watch. The
time he had taken was nearly a half second faster than
David's. 'You see,' David said, 'I tol' you I was a bit
late stoppin' it.'

Mr Reynolds had arrived by this time and checked
the watch.

'I think this watch not workin' all right,' Peter said
defensively.

'Perhaps Jet gettin' faster,' David suggested, mischievously.

'Huh! If he get any any faster we might jus' as well
forget trainin' him for a racin'-dog, 'cos nobody goin'
to have him on the track,' Mr Reynolds said with a
kind of indignation, as if he thought such speed was

somehow going to cheat him out of a good price for the puppy when he was sold. But he couldn't wait to get back home to tell his wife about the private time-trials. On the way he wanted to have the puppy near him to touch, as if he couldn't believe it was true, as if it were magic or witchcraft that made it so fast.

'Black is a gift,' the Obeahmen had told him, and David thought as he watched the dog striding along ordinary streets on the way home that Jet was somehow out of his element. He was so strong and graceful in his movement, and such a gleaming black in colour, that he made the pavements, the houses, the lamp-posts – everything they passed, including the people – look shabby and commonplace; he was like a creature from another, purer, planet.

David and Peter dropped behind their dad and let him walk both the dogs. 'It have put him in a daze, that time,' David said.

'You're tellin' me, man. It like he come up on the football pools or somethin',' Peter answered.

'Perhaps it goin' to be like that in the end,' David said, thinking again of a thousand pounds and a trip to Jamaica.

In his dream that night David went with his dad to the dog-track to watch Jet run his time-trial. He was anxious for Jet to do well.

'Go an' get the stop-watch,' his dad told him.

David didn't know where the stop-watch was. He wandered aimlessly round the back of the grandstand, not knowing where to go. In no time he was lost in a maze of huts, piles of old floodlighting, traps and mouldering timber. Every way he turned it was a dead end.

Forgetting the errand he thought only of getting back, but this was easier said than done. He met blank walls, impossible slopes, before which his legs were like lead.

Turning a corner he came to an open hut. Two men sat in the gloom inside it. David felt relief; he could ask them the way back. He approached nearer and recognized them suddenly. They were the Obeahmen. What were they waiting for? He knew the answer to the question and waited with dread, hidden behind some timbers.

When his dad came into view with Jet on the slip-lead one of the men said: 'You brought us the gift?'

'Yes, he here. You know he done well. He worth a pound if he worth a penny,' Mr Reynolds said.

'No, man, you got it wrong, remember? "Black is a gift." '

David looked on in horror as his dad walked forward to the hut to give them the dog, and the Obeahmen, smiling, stood to receive it. He tried to shout, but his voice wouldn't sound: 'No, no, you can't take him!' He struggled to rush forward, but it was no good, his dad was letting Jet go.

David struggled on and tried repeatedly to shout; but the next thing he knew he was hanging over the edge of the bed and the sheet was wrapped round his arm and trapped tightly under his body. He must have been making a noise because not only Peter but his mother was there too, trying to calm him.

When he had come fully awake and had collected himself together he understood from Peter that he had been shouting out in his sleep.

'What did I shout?' he asked.

'I dunno, man, it was all muddled, somethin' like: "Black is our gift!" and then again: "Our gift!" '

CHAPTER EIGHT

A Rainy Day

THE real trial was several months away. Meantime Mr Reynolds was very proud that they had paid off the last instalment on Allegro. Now she was his own, and she had nearly, if not quite, paid both for herself and for Jet by winning her three or four races.

Mrs Reynolds, being the cashier, kept the prize money separate from everything else. She tried not to let it dribble away in housekeeping expenses, nor even upon larger items like clothes. With Christmas coming up she saw a greater threat to the money, and hoped she would be able to cover the extra expenses without breaking into the prize money. That, she had decided, was for a rainy day.

Admittedly, she had taken on more extra work than she wanted; but by doing extra sewing, and working all the hours God sent, she found that they could cover the cost of the dogs; and it was only until Jet had his trial, showed what he could do, and fetched a handsome price; then they would make a bit of profit for all their extra work and expense.

From what her husband and the boys said she understood that Jet was a very promising dog. What that meant she didn't really know; she had read about the value of young puppies that showed great promise; but she couldn't believe the figures of sale she had seen quoted could apply to this puppy – figures in hundreds of pounds. She would be disappointed, of course, if they didn't sell him for more than twenty-five pounds; she hoped for seventy-five – that figure was within the bounds of possibility. And, if they could sell Allegro for the same, or a little more, the proceeds would make their finances look respectable and make all the effort worthwhile. Looking at the prospect realistically, though, she had decided that she would settle content with fifty pounds for the puppy – at least they would break even at that.

But her efforts to keep Allegro's winnings safe in the bank were not altogether successful. When she saw the state of the children's clothes, or considered the sameness of the food they ate, she felt that it was unfair to be too strict with her saving. She broke several times into the money, in spite of her wish to keep it whole, and the sum was gradually being whittled down; she could do nothing but sadly watch it diminish. And yet those modest family needs she worried so much about were nothing to the huge demands that were to come.

In the late summer, as a regular and specially notorious feature of the climate of the West Indies, there came from the Atlantic violent winds which in some years reached hurricane force. These hurricanes circled in the Caribbean, battering the islands before flying off and sweeping up the Eastern seaboard of the mainland of North America. The worst ones were given names, always feminine, perhaps because their character was thought to be more typically female; but the extent of the destruction these terrible storms left behind them was evidence of more than a woman's strength; the strongest Samson could never have done so much in so short a time of passage. Trees were torn up and hurled smashed to the ground; acres of crops were slashed and cut to shreds; houses were picked up, carried on a crazy aerial course to a distance far from their foundations, and pitched staggering on new ground. The force and fury of these winds was like a terrible vengeance.

David had seen photographs of this devastation; he knew it was real, though he had no memory of it. But it was not simply something he had read about in books, because he had talked about these hurricanes with his mum and dad. 'Have you really been in one? What it like?' He could not imagine it.

'Well, it too hard to tell you – jus' a great wind that bend the trees down near double to the groun', it blow in the windows, an' carry off all kind o' strange things – like a boat I seen it pick up an' perch in the top o' the trees. An' if you goes out in it you has to cling tight as you can to anythin' that fast, else you gets carried away with it too. I seen sheep an' goats blowed away like scraps o' paper,' said his dad.

'An' before it start you feels puffs of air that sort o' tell you,' his mother added, 'say: "Watch out! You can' see me but here I a-comin'." Then the air start movin' 'bout like crowds o' people in the marketplace, this way an' that, an' the sky get a funny colour like when it a thunderstorm here. But after all the threatenin' you thinks that all there goin' to be: jus' that bustle of air that put you all on edge, 'cos you waitin' an' it don't come. When all on a sudden: Wham! It come proper, an' ever'thin' go down before it. Ever'thin' strain an' groan an' cling for dear life. But it come with a roar an' while it last ever'thin' is hurtin' like a dreadful pain that won't go pass, an' that wind tug at everythin' an' even pull the roots out o' the ground it so mean.'

If the words they spoke in describing the hurricane didn't tell him the whole story, David learnt more from the expressions in their faces. As they remembered and spoke of their memories he saw the fear and strain in their eyes, and he knew that they were talking about something that came with menace and struck with evil purpose at their lives.

It was the same look David saw in his mother's eyes when she read through the letter from home in Jamaica, a letter from her mother. She announced to them all in solemn tones that a recent hurricane, 'Dora', the latest of a series that summer, had done untold damage to the family home, and that Uncle Winston had been blown off a roof where he was trying to secure the chimney against the storm. He had broken his arm and three ribs, so that he was unable even to start to repair the storm's ravages.

'My mamma say things are pretty bad, an' she been so despairin' that she haven't even had the heart to write all this long time. She don't ask for nothin' but I know we gotta help, 'cos if Winston ain't able to work I don' know what they goin' to do. We goin' to have to send somethin'.'

'Yeah, but what we got to spare?' Mr Reynolds asked, knowing very well they were talking about the money his wife had kept so safely, even in denial of their own needs.

'Well, you know I got that bit o' money from the dog-racin' that Allegro won for us.'

'Yeah, I know. How much is that?'

'Near 'nough sixty-five pound now, 'cos I had to spend on shoes an' a coat for Lotty as well as ...'

'I know how hard it have been, but you can do no other way ...'

'I can see no other way but to send some of that money home to help them. Don' you think we should?'

'I think we should. How much do you reckon we can send?'

'They're goin' to need plenty of help before they gets out of their troubles. What you think if we sends them fifty pound?'

'I think it goin' to help them quite a bit.'

And so, without delay, Mrs Reynolds sent the money order off to her family; and with Christmas so near she decided that what was left was no more than enough to make a bit of difference to their enjoyment of Christmas time, so she counted that as spent too, and planned to use it for gifts and extras for her own family.

But when she started to plan her spending, she began to feel remorse that grew stronger until she knew what she would have to do to justify herself. She went again to the post office and bought another money order, this time for seven pounds fifty. She sent it off, including a little note saying 'For Christmas', then she returned to her plans for spending her share of the money. Seven pounds fifty was not going to buy very much, and Mrs Reynolds had the most difficult task trying to decide on presents for everybody.

She tried to find out what each of them wanted, and started to ask indirect questions. With Lotty it was easy; she wanted another doll. But when she came to the others Mrs Reynolds found difficulties she

82

had not foreseen. 'What you think Pete goin' to want for Christmas?' she asked David.

'I dunno mum, but we both thinkin' of usin' our money to buy new coats for the dogs. Allegro's is all worn an' thin, an' Jet never had one. If you thinkin' of buying somethin' for me I'd rather have the money to go towards a coat for Jet.'

When she asked Peter it was the same story; he too said he'd rather that his present went towards the dogs. Mrs Reynolds was surprised, but she had another shock when she told her husband what the boys were planning, because he said he would join with them and make up the price of the coats.

Before she gave up the idea of spending the money herself, just to make sure that they were serious, Mrs Reynolds said to David: 'I had thought of buying you a book for Christmas: I seen a lovely copy of *Tom Sawyer.*'

'Oh, that *would* have been lovely, mum,' he answered, 'I should have liked that.' Regret sounded in his voice, as well as appreciation of his mother's thought, but he was steadfast and said; 'Never mind though, I can get it from the library as second best.'

After this Mrs Reynolds thought: 'When I tol' myself the money was for a rainy day I didn't mean a rainy day for them dogs!' The troubles of her family at home were the kind of thing she'd had in mind, even though those troubles were three thousand miles away. It seemed strange to her that the dogs that had for so long aggravated their poverty should be able to command the little money they had to spare at Christmas time. She wondered if the sacrifice her family seemed eager to make would ever be rewarded. She was very doubtful that it would.

CHAPTER NINE

The Price of a Gift

IT was strange and interesting to be at the dog-track in daylight when there were hardly any people about. Besides having the sense that he could look closely into everything, David felt important, being able to come here when the general public were excluded. He, Pete, and his dad were included among the small group of owners and track officials who had gathered near the paddock. Beyond the high wire, the young dogs were assembled for the time-trials.

Jet was behaving very well in the care of a kennel-maid, and his composure soothed their anxiety about how he'd be in strange company with strange handlers. But they had reckoned without the experience of the kennel staff who were so used to the work that they transferred their confidence easily even to inexperienced dogs.

Jet walked obediently whichever way he was led. David felt queer to see him muzzled, and especially so now that he was at a distance and in strange hands. The muzzle was like a piece of armour; it gave him a rather sinister and dangerous look. But he had accepted that too; he seemed very calm.

The track official had explained to Mr Reynolds what the arrangement was but David hadn't heard very clearly. He supposed one of the dogs was young like Jet and was having a trial. The other was an older

84

dog that had been put in 'to show them the way round', as the official said.

The three dogs were led straight to the start, and went into the traps without any show of temperament. The Reynoldses leaned on the rail at the end of the first straight because, Pete said, it was very important to see how Jet would take the bend – he wasn't used to running on a track. A very important difference too was in the use of the electric hare; would Jet be disturbed by the noise, and fail to start; would he run as fast as he could? As they waited, these, and other doubts, troubled them. But they needn't have worried.

The hare started, and the thin scattering of spectators looked on indifferently, for on such routine occasions it took a great deal to rouse a man's interest beyond his own dog. The promise of speed in a puppy was a very uncertain promise anyway.

The hare started, and in the daylight the sound was subdued, though the speed was undiminished. With one action six traps flew open and three dogs leapt forward in pursuit. Jet, unmistakable, though another of those three was black, seemed to be a length ahead even out of the traps. Up the first straight he opened up the gap between himself and both the other dogs. and when he passed where they stood he was more than three lengths in front.

At the bend he faltered a moment and then swung out so wide that when the positions of the dogs became clear round the other side of the track, the second dog, the adult one, had stolen ground and was a mere half-length behind. But with the straight before him Jet suddenly left the others standing and

85

streaked out one, two, three, four lengths in front, and he did it without seeming to make an effort.

There was suddenly a good deal of interest shown among the very knowledgeable watchers around the rails. Everybody looked keenly to see what this young, black dog would do at the second bend.

Jet went very wide again, and came out of the turn almost on the rails. As he came towards them it was difficult for David to decide what his position was in relation to the other dogs. When he came level it appeared that he had given ground, but his recovery was so effortless that he had kept a good lead. And now, going for the last bend, he suddenly cut inside. Increasing his speed he ran correctly, close to the inner rail; and this time when he entered the back straight he was three lengths ahead. He opened up that lead all the way to the finish.

There was a murmur all round the track. Everybody was attentive to hear the time. When it came over the loudspeaker Peter said: 'He gotta learn to take the bends!' But it was a surprising time all the same, and David saw people looking at Jet as he was brought back to the kennels. The Reynoldses followed him in and watched him led away through the paddock and out of sight. Then they stood and tried to hear the comments that were being made around them. David found the tension and excitement had left him nervous; he felt he wanted to get away from people and be on his own for a while. He walked quietly away from Peter and his dad and away from the gathering around the paddock.

As he entered the lavatory under the grandstand he

was surprised at the gloom there; nobody had bothered to switch on the lights for this daytime occasion. He could not see the faces of the two men who came in at the other entrance, but their words were clear, and what they were saying caught his attention at once. He lingered.

'He don't know a thing,' one man was saying, 'he'd take twenty-five quid for it.'

'Well, offer him thirty,' said the other.

'Thirty? I'd give three hundred if I had to – and the rest.'

'Three hundred! Well, if you're sure, give him what he asks, an' there'll be no trouble.'

'No, Fred, that's not the way. I shall baulk at what he asks because I shouldn't like him to think he's got a real class dog, should I?'

'No, but what if he asks five hundred?'

'Well, I'm not short o' that sort o' money, am I?'

'You're jokin'!'

'I was never more serious.'

'You must be pretty sure, then.'

'Sure? Sure as I ever was. That dog's got it all, an' if I don't take it off that coloured chap for seventy-five quid I'll buy you a double whisky.'

'You just wait an' see when I get him trained, there wouldn't be a ...' the buyer said, carrying the end of his sentence away with him as he and his friend went out.

David waited a few moments longer before he moved. He had stood as still as stone throughout their conversation, and he was amazed that there were people who could talk so openly with so little heed of where they were. Still, here was something to tell his dad, and without delay.

Outside, he saw that the two men were standing apart, and weren't rushing to approach his dad. He thought it safest not to let them see him coming from the direction of the lavatory, and he decided that he'd be extra careful and make a complete circuit of the grandstand so that he might rejoin his dad and Pete from the opposite direction. He kept out of sight and slid round the corner of the grandstand, congratulating himself on his cleverness.

It was only when he reached the deserted space

behind the stand, and saw the supporting timbers beneath it, the various stacks of waste, and the general untidiness, that he felt a sudden, strange anxiety that made him quicken his pace, that made him suddenly remember his dream.

But the memory was distracting; instead of hurrying now to rejoin his dad, David was possessed by an urgent curiosity to see whether the hut he remembered so clearly, that had contained the two Obeahmen, was in fact part of the scene here behind the stand. He did a rapid turn about and, half at the run, circled the area, almost willing himself to find a door into his dream.

There was only one hut, and that was in clear space; but David was so eager now to find a link that he went up to the closed door and put his hand on the latch, sure that inside he would see, if not the Obeahmen, a quality of gloom, perhaps, or some object that was familiar.

'Hey! What you want there?' The boilersuited groundsman came from the direction David had been going before his distraction.

'Nothin',' he said, and backed off, not choosing but compelled to take the way he had come as a way of escape. He could not explain that he was looking for his dream.

When he returned breathless to the place from which he had started, there was still a good number of people about, though now, with movement away from the paddock, they were more widely scattered. There was no sign of the two men he had heard talking; nor was David able to see his father and Peter.

In sudden panic, he ran to the place by the paddock

where he had left them; but there was no magic in that to bring them into view. He looked blankly on the random scattering of people, none of them even the right colour, and he was baffled. There was no explanation of their disappearance; had they gone out of the stadium, or were they here still, being cheated by those two men? David knew that was the case; he knew he had to find them and stop it. But he didn't know where to look.

Again losing control, he ran at top speed towards the gates, dodging in and out of the departing spectators. But when he came there and looked over the wide area of the car-park he could see a hundred yards, even to the stop from which they would catch the bus home, and neither his dad nor Peter was in sight.

Angry at his waste of precious time, David returned to the paddock and stood hesitant a moment, again at a loss. He saw the two men suddenly, coming from the direction of the grandstand and turning away from him towards the exit. Now he ran, not caring if he were seen, but going past them in dread of what he would learn. Well clear of them, he stopped again and saw his dad and Peter standing on the verandah of the cafe and just about to make their way down the steps. He ran.

'Dad, you haven't sold Jet?' he cried in anguish as he came up to them.

His dad turned to Pete, and they smiled at each other. 'Yes, why not? Me an' Pete jus' did good business.'

'Oh dad, you haven't let those men have him, have you?'

'Haven't I? Would you let a hundred pound go beggin', then?'

'A hundred pound! Oh, dad, you haven't, he's worth hundreds, they said so!'

'Oh! Who that, then, said so?'

David hated the self-satisfied way his dad seemed to enjoy having been cheated. In a rush he poured out the sory with his voice breaking, near to tears. 'I tried to get to tell you how much he worth but I couldn't find you,' David ended.

'You not get my message, then?' his dad asked.

'What message?' David asked, dully.

'I ask a fellah by the paddock to tell you we gone to the café.'

'Nobody tol' me. Dad, they said they'd pay five hundred pound if they had to!'

'Well, you a fine one, tellin' me that now I gone an' done what I done, ain't he, Pete?'

'You sure am, man!' Pete said. Together they enjoyed their private joke, and David looked from one to the other of them uncertainly, and said: 'Tell me, dad. What you laughin' for?'

This made them laugh more until, gaining control of himself, his dad said: 'Well, if me an' Pete had knowed them fellahs was goin' to offer five hundred pound for that pup we could have kep' them there a bit longer before we tol' them our answer.'

'What answer? What you talkin' 'bout, dad?' David guessed enough to know that the situation wasn't as grave as he had supposed.

'What I talkin' 'bout is that I didn't need them fellahs to tell me that dog worth five hundred pound.

91

That's what I sayin'.' He spoke still with amusement, yet with pride too. 'An' if I'd been dam' fool enough to want to sell him I reckon Pete here would have had somethin' to say 'bout that.'

'So you were teasin' me, you didn't sell him?' David said.

'You right there, man!' Peter told him.

And it was obvious. For the first time David was able to put himself in that situation of being approached by two strangers who wanted to take Jet away and, even worse, who wanted to cheat into the bargain.

'Tell me, tell me what happened,' David said in joy, eager to share in their joke, prepared even to be the butt of it.

'Well, we decided to have a coffee an' lef' this message for you an' then we bump into these two fellahs. The one say: "You wantin' to sell that puppy, mistah?"

' "Yes, that so, providin' the price right," I tell him.

' "Well, mistah, you got a price in mind?" he say, an' told me: "I won't lie to you, he a good lookin' dog."

'Now, I dislike the way he keep sayin' "mistah", an' talkin' as if I don't know nothin, so I say: "Well, you the expert, man, what you reckon he worth?"

' "I can tell you that in a flash," he say. "He a good dog, but he a young dog. He run a good time, but he run wide. If he change with good trainin' he might make a bit of class. But he might take up a lot more bad habits an' never win a race. My price for a puppy that have class but no solid achievement is still special. I wouldn't offer you twenty pound for that dog, no, I'd say forty, he twice as good as most."

'When he say that I jus' turn to Pete here, jus' like they weren't there, an' I say: "Well, me boy, we better be collectin' that dog an' makin' our tracks off home." An' we start off away.

'But this fellah then say: "I don't think you hearin' me all right, mistah."

' "Oh, an' what you say?" I ask him.

' "Sixty-five it was, my price."

' "Tell you the truth, man, I don' figure givin' that dog away," I say, an' me an' Pete are still movin' off.

' "Well, mistah, you better tell me your ideas," he say then, so I tell him: "My ideas makes three figures." '

They all laughed at Mr Reynolds's wit. They had barely moved from the place where David met them at the foot of the café steps.

'An' then the fellah say: "What about a hundred pound, then?" ' Here Pete took up the story: '...an' dad stay silent an' I thought for one minute he mean to take it, an' I catch his eye an' try to tell him "no".'

'You think I interested in one hundred pound?' Mr Reynolds said, turning on Peter almost in tones of anger, but joking still. 'No,' he continued, 'I lead the fellah on a bit, say: "Well now, one hundred pound a bit more 'n forty. Perhaps if we waits long enough you goin' to say two hundred, man."

' "Oh no," he tell me, "one hundred is a lot of money for an untrained dog. I'd be a fool to go any more."

' "Well, now, never mind," I say, "perhaps we can do business another time." An then me an' Pete jus' lets them see that's all we goin' to say, an' off they goes, but I reckon he haven't given up yet a while. I think he goin' to be back.'

'But dad, even if he offer you two hundred it still not enough for Jet. That dog goin' to be a real champion.' David tried his hardest to impress his dad and urge him to keep the pup. But his dad was too pleased with himself to be serious. 'Ha, I dunno what your mum goin' to say when she hear I let a hundred pound go a-beggin'. She goin' to be real mad.'

They collected Jet and made their way home. When they arrived to tell their news, they were all a bit uneasy in spite of their assurance that they were in the right.

Mrs Reynolds listened to their stories without interrupting. Then she said: 'Well, it all depend on who this man is who was so keen to buy that puppy. What do he know 'bout dogs more than we knows?'

'I can tell you who he is,' Pete said, 'he called George Chamberlain an' he got the biggest kennels in these parts. He runs dogs in all the big races.'

'An' he said he wouldn't be short of five hundred pound if he had to pay that for Jet,' David added.

'I think we goin' to see more of Mr Chamberlain,' Mrs Reynolds said, 'an' if we do it mean he is ready to give a lot of money for the puppy. An' that mean that Jet a very valuable dog. So we gotta decide pretty quick what price we want to take for him. What you think it ought to be?'

Her question took them by surprise. Without any word spoken between them the two boys and their dad had all been thinking along the same lines: if the puppy was going to be a champion dog then he ought to be their dog. Each of them had long ago dismissed the idea of taking money for him, even five hundred pounds, though that figure had certainly taken their breath away when they had first considered it. Now here was Mrs Reynolds, with her feet planted firmly on the ground, asking them to decide upon a figure at which they would sell the puppy. They didn't know how to answer her.

But Mrs Reynolds was quick to note their dismay. 'You're not – surely you don't think you're goin' to keep him!' she said.

Still no one answered her; but, though they all three remained silent, they smiled at each other like conspirators, and then mischievously, they included her. Mrs Reynolds tried to be serious but as they watched her she couldn't keep from smiling. When she smiled and tried to stop herself, they laughed, and then she was unable to resist the laughter and had to join in. The laughter grew and grew until they were helpless. Lotty, who did not understand what it was all about, went from one to the other of them trying to make them explain. But no one could explain, and they laughed more at Lotty's puzzlement, until she, hesitating at first, joined in, and was soon as helpless as the rest.

David laughed until it hurt; but it was still some time before he could stop; then he sat in a chair from weakness and was quite limp when the laughing fit was over.

'So you think you goin' to keep him,' Mrs Reynolds managed to say at last, 'but do you know enough about the trainin' to manage a dog that goin' to be a champion?'

'We knowed enough to get Allegro on the track an'

95

watch her win. You seen that,' Mr Reynolds answered. 'It goin' to be twice as easy now we got a dog that gonna win without even tryin'.'

'But what if this man come an' offer you lots of money, won't you think of takin' it 'stead of riskin' ever'thin' on that puppy-dog?'

'Huh! He goin' to offer me nothin' beside what that Jet goin' to win. You wait an' see.'

Mrs Reynolds shook her head doubtfully; but she had caught the infection; something stronger than her good sense had charmed her, and she was as excited as any of them, though she did not think it wise to let them see.

Mr Chamberlain came three nights later.

'I've come to see whether you changed your mind about that pup yet,' he said, and his tone implied that, of course, Mr Reynolds must have seen sense by this time, and would be ready to do business on reasonable terms.

'Yes, I think I have changed me mind,' Mr Reynolds answered slowly.

'Ah good, I thought you would. Now, not to beat about the bush, you just tell me what sort of price you're thinking of, an' I'll see whether I can meet you.'

'When I was at the stadium I guess I was thinkin' of five hundred pound,' Mr Reynolds said, still speaking slowly.

'Well, now that's a bit steep,' Mr Chamberlain began. 'I mean: an untried dog that ran wide at his trial...'

'But now, I changed me mind,' Mr Reynolds went on, ignoring his interruption, 'an' decided that dog ain't for sale.'

It didn't take Mr Chamberlain long to see that he was wasting his time, but he made one last try. 'Look, mister, I know how to bring that sort o' dog to the top, I've done it many times; but even with the best class dog it's still a risk. You've got to know the ropes.' He turned to Mrs Reynolds, sensing that his best hopes were in appealing to her. 'Look, mister, if you take five hundred guineas from me your problems are over an' mine have just started. What do you say to that?' He paused. Mr Reynolds did not reply. 'I've offered you the limit,' he went on, 'fair an' square. Let me take the dog, you take the money.'

'You had my answer, man,' Mr Reynolds said, 'that dog ain't for sale, not now, not ever.'

When Mr Chamberlain had gone Mr Reynolds said in a funny way, as if he was talking to himself: 'It not a right thing to give a gift away.'

CHAPTER TEN

Mr Reynolds Takes a Risk

At his introduction to the track as a serious racing-greyhound Jet didn't come up to the expectations everybody had of him. The Reynoldses all had such high hopes that they couldn't think of his failing in a mere beginners' race. They went to the track and started congratulating each other on a famous win before the race had even started. Mr Reynolds worked out how much they were going to win and said apologetically that this was only a start, nothing to the amounts to come.

But they had been disappointed; Jet had not won that first race in the class for beginners. He hadn't won, he didn't even come second or third; he had somehow failed to take the occasion seriously.

At the start he had burst out of the trap clearly ahead. Down the first straight he had increased his lead yard by yard, so that it had seemed ridiculous to match him with such competition. At the bend he was running on his own; but then, somehow, he had failed to take the narrow turn, had skidded over to the outside of the track, and had collided glancingly with the outer fence. This surprised him and stopped him for a moment before he realized that the race had left him behind, had passed him on the inside. Then he had set off in pursuit and, gamely, he had made up ground, gaining on the others and coming up to finish with the last two dogs.

'Never mind,' Mr Reynolds had tried to console them all, not least himself, 'it mean we shall have some decent odds on the next race.'

At the same meeting Allegro, whom they had tended to ignore, won a fine race and made a tidy little profit for them.

Now, on the programme at Jet's second race meeting his record did not look very impressive; they must have been the only people prepared to risk money on him. Mr Reynolds was specially anxious, though he spoke cheerfully of Jet's chances: 'He goin' to win so much it goin' to get borin' countin' it all,' he said. And to tempt them to believe this was going to be a lucky night Allegro won her race again. The prize money was twenty-five pounds: 'A good start,' Mr Reynolds said.

David sensed something in his dad's manner when Allegro's race was won. He couldn't understand what it was, but he was suspicious that his dad had a secret plan, something reckless and impatient that he daren't confess to the rest of them. David decided that he would keep an eye on him and try to prevent him from doing anything rash; there was no denying his father's extravagance. David felt that he had to guard the family interest by keeping his dad out of trouble.

Just before Jet's race Mr Reynolds said he was going to have a little flutter for them on the tote.

'I'll come with you, dad,' Peter said, sliding down from the rail where he had been sitting.

'No, you stay here, keep the places, I shan't be a minute gone,' he answered Pete shortly, and turned to make his way along to the tote.

Unnoticed, David drifted away from the others

and, going at speed, he dodged through the crowd to take up a position as close as he dared to the hatch where his dad was going to pay in his money.

With a glance about him Mr Reynolds stood at the window and pulled a roll of notes out of his pocket. He started peeling them off, one after another, standing with his hands partly hidden at the opening so that David wasn't able to count how many he paid in. But the time he took to count them off suggested that he might easily have staked the whole twenty-five pounds of Allegro's win on the doubtful chance of Jet succeeding at the second try.

David stood rooted to the spot for some seconds, but when he recovered himself he rushed forward to where his dad stood. 'Dad,' he cried, as Mr Reynolds turned from the window, 'what have you gone done?'

'Never you mind, son,' Mr Reynolds said, taken aback to see David there, 'it goin' to be all right, you see.'

'But dad, you didn't put all that money on Jet?'

'Hush boy, not a word. You see, it goin' to be fine.'

There was nothing David could do now but help share with his father the anxiety of all that money at stake; the strain of it was going to be greater for him. But they went back together to where the family was waiting, with obvious signs of impatience for the parade to start.

The world outside was dark now and still, and the night's blackness penetrated where it could into the stadium, making the contrasts between the lighted areas and the shadows more dramatic. When the dogs came out there was no place where the contrasts were so sharp as on the edge of that pool of darkness that lay in the middle of the stadium beyond the inner boundary of the track. It was there that the dogs paraded.

Six dogs and six kennel-maids did a slow circuit of the track. Jet was fourth in line, and, if the odds showed the bookmakers' lack of esteem for him, the appearance of this young dog belied the poor achievement he had made in his short racing career, and belied the bookmakers' poor views of his chances.

He was not the biggest of the dogs, but he was not overshadowed; his chest was not deeper, his legs longer or more powerful, but he had a quality – something, the Reynolds could not say what, perhaps

it was expressed in his total blackness, that made him look so splendid on the border of the Obeahland darkness. David had less reason for confidence in him than the others had; he had not shared in the hours of training they had given Jet in recent weeks to help him master the bend; but he recognized specialness in Jet as surely now as ever. The sight of the dog melting into darkness and taking shape again, with a lustre on him from the sudden angle of a light, restored David's confidence, made the dread of his father's rashness recede.

Yet as the dogs came up to the straight where the traps were set David shivered with a new wave of fear: just think if Jet were beaten by an inch and all that money was lost! But he dare not go away from the rails as he would have liked to do, and miss the race altogether. He looked at his dad and saw signs of the same anxiety in his face. He was pretending very hard to look confident, but David saw sweat moistening his hairline. There was nothing for it but to stay; what would the others say if he were to miss the race? They'd think he was ill and that would spoil things for them.

But he was ill! Things *were* spoilt for him. This was the last time he would have anything at all to do with putting bets on. For a fleeting moment, before he drove the thought out of his mind, he imagined what his mum would say if his dad had to confess that he had lost all the prize money from Allegro's race. His mind was in a turmoil, he couldn't concentrate on anything about him; he was bewildered by the bustle and excitement, and he stared straight ahead, seeing nothing.

Pete and his mother pressed themselves close to the rail side by side. Lotty heaved herself up on her elbows to see better, and her tiptoes tried to find a hold on the lower boards; they were all silent, each in his own way trying to contain the excitement.

The dogs were in the traps now, and they waited for the sound of the hare starting his run. Once that began, the rest was fast and furious. The hare drew the dogs out of the traps and the race was on.

'Swoosh!' There it was, the sound that electrified the whole scene, spectators and all. They saw the lop-eared little creature making his challenge to the dogs, his yellow colouring attracting their notice and his speed inciting them to fury in the tiny cages where they strained to hurl themselves forward in pursuit.

He went once round the track and, as he passed the traps the second time, he was moving very fast, though still one ear waved calmly up and down. With a clash the traps shot open, and the dogs, all six, clawed their way out into free space and tried to find and settle into their strides. A black dog, near the centre, spearheaded their rush; and he drew that spear-point out and tapered it sharper as he drew further ahead. Passing their part of the rail Jet was way out in front. David, shouting, heard his father say: 'Two lengths, now go inside for the bend.'

From behind, they saw Jet cut across to the inside rail, but he did not go far enough for Mr Reynolds. 'Further! further!' he called. And on the bend itself Jet must have been troubled, for when they came clear in the opposite straight, his lead was cut, the other dogs, the next leaders, were bunched close on his heels.

'He floats, drifts over too far at the bend!' Mr

103

Reynolds shouted in frustration to anyone who would hear. 'His speed throw him wide.'

But the straight was no problem; here, in no time, Jet seemed to leave the rest standing as he pulled away again to uncrowded space. He was two – three – four lengths ahead before the final bend. Here the watchers were unable to guess what was happening in the changing perspective.

The group of dogs wheeled round into the final straight, and David saw their positions. He shouted 'Jet!', uttering his first word since the race had begun, and that was a word of triumph. Jet was four lengths ahead. Mr Reynolds told them afterwards that he had lost nothing on the turn. But four lengths wasn't good enough for Jet, and in the home straight he stepped it up to five, according to the official result.

Peter and David stood looking at the tote board for the announcement of the payment. 'If Pete only knew how much we goin' to collect,' David thought, 'how much we might have lost!' He was pale and felt feeble from the strain he had suffered, and even now they had won he couldn't easily unwind. He felt weary, and wanted only to get home, to sit, and to try to relax.

Mr Reynolds didn't say a word about his dealings with the tote. He went to collect his winnings, and on the way home he laughed and talked, making puzzling little remarks that pleased him, though no one else understood; David alone knew they referred to the huge winnings he had collected. But he kept quiet, he knew his dad wanted to enjoy his secret, and he hadn't the spirit himself to do more than plod home and flop into a chair when he arrived.

Mrs Reynolds made some coffee, and when they were all sitting round enjoying it David saw his dad preparing to declare his success.

'Now Barbara,' he said, 'I goin' to show you a surprise.'

When Mrs Reynolds and the boys were attentive – he had waited until Lotty had been sped off to bed – he brought out a great fistful of notes from his back pocket and counted them out on the table. 'There you are,' he said proudly, 'hundred and fifty pound!'

'Where you get that money?' Mrs Reynolds asked in alarm.

Patiently, he explained the sum: the prize money from Allegro's win, the same from Jet's, 'An' the rest come from a little flutter I had on the tote.'

'Little flutter!' she cried. 'You mean to say you won a hundred pound on that puppy-dog's race?'

'That jus' right.'

'An' pray, where you get that sort o' money – you didn't use Allegro's prize money?'

Mr Reynolds was less sure of himself now, but he grinned mischievously, and nodded. 'That's right, I did,' he confessed, still pleased with himself. With the spread of notes on the table he thought he could receive his wife's scolding and enjoy it. But at the end of it all Mr Reynolds was almost sorry he'd been so foolish; his wife had a way with words, and, in spite of his happiness to be able to give her so much, she made him realize what the story might have been.

'What would you have found to say for yourself, I wonder, if you had robbed Allegro, who near run her heart out for you, robbed her of all that money she won? I hear you talkin' 'bout gifts; that money was

105

her gift to you, an' you don't care no more 'bout her gift than to go 'n bet with it on a dog that haven't hardly been on the race-track before. I thought that was the mos' foolish thing when you brought racin'-dogs here in the first place, but now you startin' with foolishness worse than anythin' I ever seen. I tell you, Shirland Reynolds, if you does anythin' like that again I goin' to get that Mr Chamberlain an' I goin' to pay him to take them dogs away from you 'cos you ain't fit to have 'em.'

David was relieved when it ended, because he was afraid that his mum might know in some uncanny way that he was a bit guilty, and tell him off for not stopping his dad. Bt when he saw he was safe he was glad that it had happened, for such risks as his dad had taken frightened him. He knew his mum's disapproval was the best discouragement against it happening again.

CHAPTER ELEVEN

Under the Weather

AFTER Jet's career as a racing dog had been success-fully launched, the activities of training continued the same. There was no change at the kennels, for the conditions at the house didn't permit any change; but Mr Reynolds and Pete took extra care now with the feeding and the grooming and the exercising of the dogs.

Jet began to have a success on the track that was uncanny. He ran four further races at the local sta-dium and won them with ease. David had been un-able to attend any of these meetings because they were mid-week ones; but what he learnt from his dad and Pete was that the betting prices had changed race by race, and it was now impossible even to double your money by backing Jet.

'You needs to put fifty pound on him to have a decent win,' Pete told him.

'Is that what dad been doing?' David asked, fearing that the effect of his mother's scolding had worn off already.

'Oh no, he don' dare risk so much even though Jet keep winnin'. I think he never go more 'n ten pound.'

That seemed a huge sum to David, but he had to consider that Jet's performance seemed to justify these higher stakes. 'Does mum know he put so much on?' he asked.

'I think she have made an agreement with him that

he can go so high till he lose, then he gotta put less on.'

Mr Reynolds decided to move Jet from the local stadium to the larger one at Brent City where he was unknown, and where the competition would be stiffer. They wouldn't be able to go and see him so often; but it wasn't such a bad state of affairs as they might imagine, he told them consolingly, because when you had a dog that was exceptional you expected it to outclass every other dog on the local track; the real excitement and the real money was to come – if Jet was really the dog they took him to be.

But there was no hurry to rush him into the big competition, Mr Reynolds said – the Greyhound Classics. He was young yet; it would be dangerous to push him too hard; he needed a good deal more experience and middle-class competition before he went in for anything more taxing. 'But,' Mr Reynolds said, 'if all go well, next year we might go try him at one of the real big tracks.'

'Where are the big tracks?' asked David.

'Oh, in London.'

'An' what about the big races – the Classics?'

'Oh yes, he goin' to win all those,' Mr Reynolds said, laughing, 'but there are other good races he might try first – the Midland Trophy for one – he still young, but he goin' to take all these races in his stride.'

David, like Lotty, still felt something for Jet which had nothing to do with his specialness as a racing dog. From the first, when Jet was new-born, David had wanted to make him a pet. But at first he had been too valuable to pet, and now his life was too busy and important for there to be any question of playing with him. Indeed it was even becoming difficult to see him, for he spent days away at the track, and when he was at home he had to be allowed to rest, so that at their rare meetings David was only able to admire his beauty, and feel from a distance that warmth he couldn't let himself express.

Besides, there was the mystery about Jet that was still quite chilling. When David looked into his face, or saw him moving at exercise, he was aware of a strange, withdrawn spirit that was unlike anything he found in Allegro. Jet's sleekness and the darkness of his eyes expressed it, and thinking about this David realized that some of the names he had thought of showed a recognition of this spirit. 'Shadow', he had named him, and 'Pluto, King of the Underworld'. Jet was like a king, a royal dog, he was proving that.

Mr Reynolds's way of recognizing this was to improve the security of the yard and the kennel. He fixed a new, stronger padlock on the kennel door, a bolt on the backyard gate, and he raised wire three feet high on top of the old wall that surrounded the yard. 'You can't be too careful when you got a dog that worth so much money,' he said. And Mrs Reynolds and the boys noticed that he was very reluctant to leave the house empty; he was always making inquiries about who was going to be in and who was going out during the time that he would be at work. In the evenings he took up the habit of strolling out and doing tours of the yard.

'You'll have to get Securicor in, dad, with Alsatian dogs to tear any intruders to pieces,' David suggested. But it was not a subject for joking with his dad; Mr

Reynolds looked at him deadly serious and said: 'Yes, I been thinking I might need somebody to watch when there ain't no one at home.'

And yet it was Jet, the reason for his concern, who was least at home these days. Since his racing scene had moved to Brent, he often stayed in the kennels on the track, and they didn't see him for a week at a time. His 'star' quality wasn't altogether as exciting to them as they had thought it would be. Mr Reynolds missed him as much as the rest of them.

Jet was winning races, of course, what else? But the action was so far away that they didn't feel themselves part of it; and even if Mr Reynolds and sometimes Pete went to see Jet run, the rest of them didn't share in the triumphs. When they heard the outcome of the race, it was just another win, they had no idea of how it had gone.

One day David, on his way home from school, went more eagerly than usual because he expected Jet to be home. He broke into a run over the last hundred yards, and his first words to his mother were: 'Is Jet back?'

'Yes, he is,' she answered, 'but I'm afraid he not very well. The vet have been an' he say it a stomach upset, some bug he pick up at the stadium. He there.'

It was the unexpectedness of having Jet lying in the house in a blanket in the place where he had been born that had prevented David from seeing him at once. Pete nodded his permission from the chair in which he had watched over the birth, and David went up close.

Jet opened his eyes to him, and the tail that stuck out from the blanket tried, but didn't quite manage, to wag. Now, however, he did not look very regal; his eyes seemed to squint, and they looked very pained. From time to time he made alarming retching noises, and once he tried to raise himself, but the effort was too much. After that momentary flicker of interest at David's approach, he had withdrawn into himself, closing his eyes and lying prone. He was further away than when he was at the Brent City Stadium.

'Will he be all right?' David asked, kneeling beside him and touching lightly on the dog's sleek head.

'The vet say it a matter of time,' his mum answered, 'it a serious, but not uncommon trouble. He a strong dog, an' he should pull through all right. We shall jus' have to wait.'

David was troubled, anxious, appalled at the thought that danger could threaten Jet, this gifted dog, winner of all his races – but that very first one. Could so great a gift of speed survive such an illness? The difference between Jet and other dogs was so slight and yet so crucial. Though greyhounds were built for speed, this one had so perfect a balance of the qualities needed that he was speedier. Such an illness might do some harm to upset that balance, David thought, and the mere possibility of it struck him with dread.

And it was not only that Jet was their dog; it was the thought that a rare gift of speed might be taken away. The only thing anyone could do was wait and let Jet battle with the sickness; but that was not easy waiting. David found he could relieve the anxiety a little by making a fuss of Allegro; but then Mrs Reynolds said they must be extra careful so as not to pass the germs on to Allegro. Not only had they to wash their hands before preparing and giving her her food; but they must keep away from her, too, as much as possible.

Pete sat over Jet patiently; Mr Reynolds found the sickness so hard to bear that for three days and nights he didn't know what to do with himself. Sometimes in the evenings he became so upset to look on helpless and see the dog lying listless and weak that he had to go out and tramp the streets to relieve his tension. It was his dread too that this gift, given by chance, might suddenly be taken away from them as inexplicably as it had come.

Lotty was like the rest of them, full of baffled concern. She would crouch on her heels over the dog as he lay, and murmur her words of consolation, because she knew she had neither to touch nor to speak. Suddenly, on the fourth day, as they were all sitting in heavy silence, a silence that had lain like fog over their world throughout Jet's illness, Lotty, crouching there, said with a startling clarity: 'He licked my hand.'

She held up her hand, and Mr Reynolds looked at it as if he expected to see the evidence there, printed upon it. 'Did he do that?' he asked eagerly.

'Yes, look.' Lightly, she stroked Jet, and they all saw his tail wag with more liveliness than they had seen for days. He raised his head and Lotty laid it on her knee to stroke him. Mr Reynolds was about to intervene when his wife put out a restraining hand and held him. Together, they watched Lotty revive the dog's interest, and they saw the gleam come again into his eye.

'Perhaps he want to take a drink o' water, Pete,' Mr Reynolds said, and Peter brought a dish of fresh water, which Jet, raising himself up on his forepaws, drank at thirstily.

The signs of improvement were good signs. Soon Jet was on his feet, moving about, showing interest. It took several days for Mr Reynolds to trust the signs, and he wouldn't let the dog out of his sight when he was at home. Peter had the strictest instructions to watch over him the rest of the time. At last, even his doubts were cleared, and he and Peter began to take Jet out again for mild exercise, letting him off the lead for only a short time. Though Mr Reynolds continued to watch fearfully for signs of weakness, he gradually accepted that Jet was recovered and anxious to be himself again.

The vet said he must be kept on a light schedule for a fortnight, however, and so the children, even Lotty, were able to play with him on his walks and make a fuss of him. They stroked and patted him, and encouraged him to play, and for them and for the dog this affection given and returned was new, different from anything there had been in the relationship before, even when Jet was a puppy. Lotty knelt beside him with her arms round his neck and said: 'I wish I could keep you like this. I wish you were mine.' And David felt the same thing, regretting the return to the strict routine that was to come at the end of Jet's convalescence.

Mrs Reynolds watched through the kitchen window and said: 'The children have helped that dog over this illness.'

'Yes,' said her husband, 'I think you right.'

'An' I don't think that bit o' spoilin' goin' to do him any harm at all – you see.'

'I wonder,' Mr Reynolds said. He had not lost all his dread of the illness; he wanted to see Jet return to his full racing form before he would be reassured.

'Oh, I think you goin' to find it done him good. An' if I'm right, you know what I think you ought to do in future?'

'What that?'

'I think you must bring him back here after the races. Never mind how far it is, let him come back to see the children.'

Peter had gone out now into the yard, and as the parents watched, Jet came bounding up to him and leapt up at him in play. Then he raced from one to the other of them blithely.

'I think he frets away from here – an' specially away from Pete. Perhaps that what put him under the weather.'

'Well, I can see no harm, you usually right. If I get him back in winning form that's what I goin' to do.'

They went out now into the yard, and Jet came prancing up to welcome them. His coat shone again and rippled with vitality, and his eye was clear.

CHAPTER TWELVE

The Midland Trophy

By the time he date of the Midland Trophy came up, Jet had run two races and had won them both. The signs were clearly in favour of his readiness.

'When the race is run we all goin' to be there,' Mr Reynolds said, defying his wife to say any different.

'What?' she said with disapproval of such extravagance. 'You mean we all goin' to go all that way to Brent jus' for that, twenty mile?'

'That's right. We all goin' to see that dog win,' he answered smiling, and when that special Friday came they did go.

What surprised David about the grand stadium at Brent was that, though it was built to accommodate much larger numbers than the local stadium, it was not any more luxurious or expensively fitted out. The concrete steps had been as roughly cast to make this larger grandstand; the bookmakers worked more busily with the same simple furniture; and the only real differences were of scale.

Even the programme was much the same, with six preliminary races leading up to the big race that came last on the bill. No one was much interested in the earlier races – in fact, the first one was over when they arrived; and as they took their places in the stadium the second race was about to start.

It failed to capture anyone's interest, however. Mr Reynolds didn't even trouble to pick a winner, and when the race was over he suggested they go to the cafe to pass the waiting time in more comfort.

The excitement of the next two races came to them in glimpses they caught indifferently through the wide window, and from the bursts of frenzied shouting that accompanied the running. Each time, David noticed, it was the same pattern.

One more to go. The dogs paraded. The hare was started. Then, suddenly, there was a different character to the shouting in this race: not simply excitement, but cries of astonishment, dismay, amusement, coming separately from the crowd. The boys were drawn by curiosity to see what was happening; but it was over almost before they could move.

'Funniest thing I've ever seen,' a man said to the room in general, as he entered the cafe. 'The dogs got snarled up all in a lump, and the one that got free won by a mile!'

'An' that what Jet goin' to do in the nex' race: win by a mile!' said Mr Reynolds.

'You shouldn't count your chickens, Shirland Reynolds,' his wife said, teasing.

He laughed confidently. 'Maybe not, but you never seen the likes of him. I never see a dog run like him, an' never see a dog with his nature. He a knowin' dog; ain't nothin' goin' to stop him winnin'.'

Now they went out onto the track to find their places, and with the tension building Mr Reynolds began to talk more cautiously.

'I think you goin' to see a fair race,' he said, 'because all the dogs here' – he pointed to the details on the race-card – 'are somethin' special. I hear one or two of 'em fancied, an' this one in particular: Shootin'

116

Star. Jet ain't home yet, you goin' to have a real race between these two. Now, you like to have a little flutter on this one, Barbara? Break a rule?'

'How much you say that dog goin' to win if he come first?'

'Seven hundred fifty pound is the prize money.'

'Then I think I be happy to settle for that. But you go an' make a bet, I know you like to have somethin' at stake.'

'It make the race more excitin',' Mr Reynolds said with a twinkle in his eye, pleased that his wife had entered into the spirit of the occasion enough to accept that it was part of the sport to have a bet. He went off happily to arrange it.

The announcement over the loudspeaker began as Mr Reynolds returned. It was suitably solemn, for this was one of the very important races outside the Classics. The prize was a cup with a value of two hundred and fifty pounds, and with the cash prize the winner stood to gain handsomely.

Now the dogs were being announced, and at the same time they came from the paddock with the kennel-maids. Interest in hearing the descriptions faded as the dogs, muzzled and wearing their colours, entered through the rail and crossed the track to begin their walk round the inside, the long way round to the start.

There was first Miss Otis, a beautiful, slender, fallow bitch; she was followed by Corner Boy, a fawn dog; Ricky Rum came third, his greyness shading to blue under the belly in this light; fourth was Hot Pepper, a brindle; and Shooting Star, a sooty black, preceded Jet, whose coat shone, seeming to draw the light. The rivals were fifth and sixth.

'How beautiful he is!' Mrs Reynolds said. 'This is where he look his best. It almost as if he have power to turn on a light inside when he step on the track.'

The dogs stretched in line, going leisurely down the long reach opposite. They entered the bend and came slowly round to the traps and the start. The bustle and the lively chatter gave way to a stiffening of the ranks along the rail, and to a subdued murmur of voices as the tension mounted. David, with both hands clutching the rail, felt his palms hot and moist as he waited. He wanted to speak to ease the huge excitement, but he was compelled to surrender himself to the atmosphere of expectation which demanded that he be quiet and still. He pressed himself close to the rail to hold in the agony of waiting.

'I hope he gets off fast,' he was thinking. 'What if his trap stuck an' he didn't get away properly? That wouldn't be fair. But it couldn't happen, they'd know. The race would have to be run again. Oh let him win!'

Without knowing why, David thought of Gbeah as a power that could work for Jet's success, and, as he realized this, he saw Jet stalking the fringe of that blackness where he seemed half of the element of light, half of darkness. 'And he has the best of both of them,' David thought, 'understanding and magic.'

He felt no charity towards the other dogs in the race, however. 'Shooting Star can get baulked, just let Jet run clear, an' it don't matter what happen behind him. Let them all run – behind.'

His thought somehow overran the moment when the hare started; and he was startled, incredulous, when he realized that the long, tense wait was over. A

118

new tension seized him, taking hold as the noise of the hare began. But the hare seemed to travel for fifty yards at a snail's pace. It was like watching the second hand of your watch: the slowcoach that you willed to go faster. And then the hare did move faster; it zipped by them even though their impatience made it seem a dawdle.

There was an explosion, sharp and loud upon the underlying electric hum, as the traps were sprung and the dogs burst out and streaked into the straight. They came as a torrent, and the tension of the crowd broke in shouts of encouragement everywhere around the track: 'Miss Otis! My beauty!' 'Run, Ricky Rum!'

And it was a wild confusion of noise as the dogs came past them. The instant impression was of a jagged line like a flash of lightning.

'Jet! Jet!' they cried, with desperate anxiety, for they could not tell his place; it was all too fast; and the dogs were so close that his position did not register. Was the real competition going to be too testing for him?

Into the bend and a flurry of heels and flying turf that gave no way of knowing who led; there was only the sense of effort as the dogs bent their motion slowly, like iron bars, back into the straight at the further side. A black dog had thrust himself half a length up on the others.

'Shooting Star!' a man's voice yelled from nearby, sounding loud and clear above the din, so that David's hopes took a lurch from his confidence. Down the straight the dog went clear; 'Jet!' they all shouted, 'Jet!' It must be him.

There was one dog trailing, then a bunch of three,

119

and then in front were two black dogs, each with clear space behind him, each drawing that space out. Into the bend, and the colours of the leading dogs were plain. David sweated, he couldn't remember which was which, and he couldn't take his eyes off the race to check his card.

'Jet!' Pete cried, but his voice was so strained that there was no telling whether it was anguish or joy he expressed.

'Come on, boy!' Mr Reynolds shouted, somewhere, high over David's head, and he thought he heard a reassurance in that. The dogs were out of the bend, the hare raced ahead of them. But the dog that led was in an element of his own. He was like some dark planet arcing effortlessly through space. There was no other that could stay with him, for they could not

enter his element. Their grunts and pantings behind were their tribute to him.

'Jet!' all the Reynolds cried, loud in praise, as he followed his course into the last turn and went for the line. Shooting Star crossed three lengths behind, and then came Miss Otis.

'He have run a classic race!' Mr Reynolds cried, 'an' them others really helped him run.'

CHAPTER THIRTEEN

Lost

'WHAT'RE you readin'?' a man's voice asked as David walked out of the house on his way to the library. He had given no attention to the G.P.O. van that was parked outside the door; now he looked up in the direction of the voice, and saw a youngish man with long hair smiling down at him from a ladder reared up against a telegraph pole. The man was working with pliers among the complicated connections, and David saw for the first time that there was a branch wire going from this pole through a gap between two houses and somewhere round the back.

He held up his book. *'Tom Sawyer,'* he said.

'Hm!' the man answered, impressed. 'I like a good read meself. Got stacks o' books at home – adventure, jungle stories, that sort o' thing. You interested in that?'

'Yes,' said David, politely.

'Bring you some next time I'm round this way; which house do you live in?'

'That one,' David said, pointing, 'number seventeen.'

'Is that the one with the telegraph pole in the back yard?'

'No,' David answered, uncertain, 'the greyhounds.'

'Oh yes,' the man answered without any show of interest.

'We've got the fastest dog in England,' David went

on, hurt by his new friend's indifference, and determined to impress him.

'Get away!' the man answered, teasing.

'It's true. He was first in the Midland Trophy last
month, an' he goin' to win all the Greyhound Classics
next year.'

'Bet he'll get beat in his first race,' the man said,
'when he comes up against the real competition.'

'Huh!' David scoffed. 'You look out for him, he's
black, that's why ...'

'I bet you'll be tellin' me you train him next,' the
man said, maddeningly.

'I do,' said David. 'Well, I help.'

'Stroll on! That Jet needs very careful handling; it
wants a professional for that.'

'Me an' my brother go up to the park every week to
help me dad with the dogs.'

'I'll believe you, hundreds wouldn't.' The man
banged on the wire with his pliers and shouted, 'Any
good?'

'It's a cinch,' a voice answered from somewhere
along the wire round the back of the houses.

'Well, I'll be goin' on,' David said, awkwardly,
since the man was apparently again involved in his
work.

'Yes, righto old friend. I'll bring you them books
round.'

'Thanks, so long,' David said.

When he came to the end of the street he turned to
look back at the G.P.O. man, but there was no sign of
him; even the ladder and the van were gone. 'Huh!'
he thought. 'It couldn't have been much if they've
finished so soon. I wonder if he will bring me some

books.' With this thought David went on his way to the library and forgot all about the G.P.O. man and his books; the library was of more immediate interest.

The next day but one Pete went out to the kennel as usual to see the dogs. Allegro met him at the back door, and, just as he was asking himself who was supposed to lock up last night, he noticed that the hasp had been unscrewed from the door jamb and the door opened without the lock being disturbed. Jet was not inside the kennel; he was not in the yard. Pete ran to the gate at the bottom. It was closed, but not bolted.

He ran back to the house calling, 'Dad! Dad!' and bursting in he shouted: 'Jet have been stolen. He gone, vanished.'

All the family rushed out to the backyard; but it was no good looking there, the bare yard offered no place where a dog could hide. When they had made this simple, useless gesture of concern, nobody knew what to do or to say; they were paralysed, struck dumb.

The police asked for clues – anything that might lead to the thieves. Nobody could help; it seemed such simple wickedness to steal their dog that none of them could imagine anyone capable even of thinking of it. But then Mrs Reynolds remembered Mr Chamberlain, who had shown such enthusiasm to buy the dog, and such frustration when he had failed. She mentioned this to the police sergeant, and her husband leapt at the suggestion, and was immediately convinced that the case was solved.

'Yes, I've heard of Mr Chamberlain,' the sergeant said soberly, 'and of course we have to follow up any line of enquiry. We'll naturally check with all the local kennels, but I'm sure you understand that we'd have to go very carefully with this one. I hope you won't let Mr Chamberlain's name be mentioned outside this room.'

With a look Mrs Reynolds made her husband hasten to agree.

But there was something about his memory of Mr Chamberlain that didn't fit David's feeling about the theft. He racked his brains to understand why, and he had a picture of Mr Chamberlain as a big, stout, middle-aged man, while he thought of the thief as being younger, slighter and – long-haired. Then, just as the policemen were going, he told the story of the G.P.O. man. And even as he was telling it he realized something. 'When I said we had this great dog he pretended not to believe me or to be interested, but then he said its name, "Jet", before I'd told him.'

'Yes,' the sergeant said, 'that sounds like a possible lead. These men – you say you didn't see the other – could well have been collecting data for a break-in. We'll follow it up, and we'll let you know of our progress.'

Mr Reynolds wasn't satisfied with the way the police were carrying out their investigations. He wasn't satisfied because two days had passed and Jet wasn't yet returned to him. There was no promise of a return. He and Peter and David spent their time in vain wanderings around the town, hanging about the track and the kennels of the owners they knew; it was a pointless search, and merely a way of occupying themselves.

As they walked down one street in an unfamiliar area Mr Reynolds suddenly said something, which

David didn't catch, about 'askin' a fellah I know ...'
He urged them to move on and then stopped himself
to knock upon a door. The boys loitered, kicking at
the kerb; they were both fed-up of asking and getting
no answers, and of wandering. But this time David
was arrested by the appearance in the doorway of a
man with long black hair; and though he heard not a
single word that his father spoke, nor any given in
answer by the man, he knew that as a way of finding
Jet his Dad meant to consult Obeah again. This was
the assistant of the Obeahman.

When they all three continued on their way David
looked at his dad and said, 'Anythin'?'

'No, he don' know nothin'.'

But David knew that he had a date, perhaps that
evening, and must keep a watchful eye on his dad's
movements.

It was a black night when David followed his father
at a safe distance down the street towards their ap-
pointment. Of course, his dad had made an excuse to
go out alone, and David had prepared a suitable explanation of his own hasty departure immediately
upon his dad's heels. Speed was necessary, because he
could not count on the second meeting with Obeah
being in the same derelict street.

But there, it seemed, was his dad's destination; and
David followed carefully, but sufficiently close to
observe any possible sudden change of direction. In
fact the route was familiar – his dad went to the same
house as before. David knew what to do.

As he entered the front door and turned inside, he
saw a glint of light from the back; but this time when

he went through into the kitchen he found that the men surrounded not a brazier, but a simple candle standing on a brick in the shelter of the wall of the outbuilding. Taking up a comfortable position in which to watch, David first saw the men passing the rum bottle round to each other in leisurely style as they squatted. The Obeahmen were against the wall, his dad was in the open; but they were all close up to the candle, so that it lit their faces weirdly, and sent shadows shooting as they moved. There was a mumble of voices as before, though again David could hear no words clearly.

After a while passed in this manner the ritual began in a simple, matter-of-fact style. The men stood, and while his dad and the long-haired man leaned against the wall of the outbuilding, the third man first set out his bricks, and then did his spinning action, starting slowly, and working up rapidly to frantic speed. Without concern for his person he fell once again like a log, motionless on the ground.

'Now, if you there – yeah, I think he there, he have give me the sign – if you there I say: man here want to know 'bout his dog gone been took away. I axin' you 'bout that dog been stole. Is you goin' to say anyt'ing 'bout that?' Each part of the long-haired man's speech was followed by a pause, but even then, it was some time before there was a response.

Day is white,
An' black is the night.
Ever'thin' goin' to be all right,

came the strange, strangled utterance from the body on the ground.

127

'Is that what you gotta tell him? Does you want to tell this fellah any mo' 'bout that dog been stole?'

The strange little verse was repeated.

'All done?' asked the first man.

'All done!' the voice came, sounding mean and rather cross when pressed further.

'There, you hear what he say. He say ever'thing gonna be all right.'

David was astonished by the verse. It didn't mean any more to him than it did to his dad, who was letting the man know that he wasn't very much enlightened by it; but, unlike his dad, David recognized an echo in the verse of something in his own thought. Sometime, recently, he'd had that same image in his mind: 'Day is white, And black is the night' – what could it mean?

But there was no time to ponder it now. Rather more doubtful than he had been last time, Mr Reynolds was preparing to take leave of the Obeahmen. 'You sure it goin' to be all right?' he was saying to the man who was now on his feet, recovered from the trance.

'You want to ask Obeah mo' questions you gotta pay, man,' he was told.

'Don' worry, you hear what he say: it gonna be all right,' the other man said consolingly.

And Mr Reynolds had to accept that reassurance and make his way home, going, as before, down the narrow passage at the side of the house. Almost at once, when he had disappeared, one of the men dowsed the candle, and they followed, making David safe to leave the dark and unwholesome kitchen where twice now he had received messages that seemed meaningless, yet of which the first, 'Black is a gift',

128

had been proved to contain a truth. He went away now and tried to apply the words of this second message to their problems. He did not have any success.

It was now a week since Jet had disappeared. The police offered no promise of solving the mystery and Mr Reynolds was cast in gloom.

'What you done 'bout that Mr Chamberlain – you been to see him?' he asked the sergeant.

'We made routine inquiries, that's all we can do without further grounds for investigation,' the sergeant answered, stiffly. 'Mr Chamberlain claims he has no knowledge that would help us, and that, in the circumstances, is what we must accept. You give us a more definite lead, and we'll certainly follow it up. Oh, by the way, that G.P.O. van – it was stolen. It was found abandoned and of course we're going over it, checking for fingerprints and everything. I'll keep you informed, Mr Reynolds.'

When he had gone Mr Reynolds grumbled at the failure of the police to do anything useful. 'I think I goin' to start some investigations on me own,' he said. 'I goin' to see that Chamberlain fellah an'...'

'Oh no you're not! What good you think that goin' to do, 'cept to make a fool of yourself?' his wife said. 'You think he goin' to have that dog there on show? If he have stolen him you bet he not goin' to let you or anyone else have sight of him to say: "That my dog." You leave it to the police, Shirland Reynolds, that your only way.'

Peter didn't say very much about Jet's disappearance; but he never did say very much, anyway, and

David knew that it was Pete more than any of them who was grieved by the loss. And that was not surprising since Jet had given Pete something that was very important to him: an occupation, and the work Jet's care involved him in had been stolen away from him with the dog.

But, because Pete considered the care of Jet to be his job, he had been busier than anybody – the police included – in trying to trace Jet, trying to pick up some clue that would lead to the discovery. He had spent all the time, day-long, since Jet's disappearance, wandering aimlessly, not knowing where to look, but compelled to look somewhere.

David knew how Peter searched, and he asked for a full report each evening when Peter and he were alone. David asked if he could go along on the Saturday when he was free of school. He decided that when he went there should be a plan and some purpose in the search: they would go and have a look at Chamberlain's place.

Pete was agreeable, but not quite as keen on the idea as he would have been if he had not already visited the Chamberlain kennels himself, and with no useful result. But David was determined; there was no other plan he could propose.

'What did you do when you went?' David asked Peter as they travelled out of town to the suburbs that bordered the countryside where Chamberlain's kennels were situated.

'I jus' walked round it. It have a high wire fence all round. I kep' out of sight an' I hide in a wood that is close to the kennels an' I look out for Jet,' Peter answered. 'But there ain't no dog there that I knows.'

130

David let Peter guide him off the road and along a hedge into the little wood from whose cover they were able to look in through the wire on the expensive layout that Chamberlain had provided for his dogs. There was a number of wooden sheds regularly spaced at one end of the enclosure, and the rest, the part furthest from the house, was a spacious area of grass in which the dogs could exercise. Several of them ran and sported in this area as the boys watched; but the journey was wasted as a search for some sign of Jet.

Mr Chamberlain appeared and did some work among the sheds, but there was no other interest in the scene before them. Even David was ready to leave when they had spent an idle half-hour watching these strange dogs leisurely at play.

'But where do they train?' David asked, suddenly.

'Trains at the track, I suppose,' Peter answered, without interest.

'No, they don't. I'm sure I've seen it on the race-card that Chamberlain train his own dogs ... I think I got a card here.' He fumbled eagerly through his pockets.

'This what you wants?' Peter pulled a crumpled race-card from his own pocket. David seized it and opened it feverishly to search out the information. 'Yes, there you are,' he said, triumphantly, pointing to the proof. Chamberlain's dogs were trained by the owner away from the stadium.

'Well, where he go? Perhaps in the fields near here,' Pete said, not thinking too much about the question. Getting a clue to Jet's whereabouts was much more important to him than knowing where Mr Chamberlain trained his dogs.

'But do you think that likely?' David asked. 'Do you think Chamberlain do his trainin' like us with an old bike somewhere? I think he have another posh place – I don' know where – but if he have Jet it very likely he have him where he can see what that dog can do. He gotta keep him in trainin'.'

Peter began to show interest. 'Where you think he have this place?'

'I don' know, but I think I know how to find out. Come on.'

David led the way, and he didn't stop until they reached home.

His mother was in the house alone, which was exactly what David wanted. He explained to her what they'd seen, and told her of his idea about Chamberlain's having another place somewhere where he trained his dogs. 'We want to find out if he has and where the place is,' he said.

'The phone book?' Mrs Reynolds suggested.

'No good, I've looked. It only give the kennels number.'

'Well, what then?' she asked, puzzled.

'I wondered if you could ring up the Greyhound Stadium, say you very anxious to speak to Mr Chamberlain, but you couldn't get him at the kennels; could they tell you where his trainin' place is an' give you the number?'

'Huh! Why me?' Mrs Reynolds asked.

'Well, you got a posh English accent when you want to use it. Nobody'd suspect you of wantin' to steal back a dog from him.'

When Mrs Reynolds stepped out of the phone-box the boys looked at her expectantly. She had refused to let them come in to hear her posh English accent, and now her face gave nothing away.

'Well, mum, come on, tell us,' David said.

'What is it exactly that you want to know?' she asked in her posh English accent.

'Where Chamberlain train his dogs. Oh, come on, mum,' David urged.

'Mr Chamberlain the owner?' she went on, 'Oh yes, just one moment. That's right, it's not the kennels you want, here we are: Berkley 473 is the number, and the address is "White Bricks", Berkley Common.'

'Berkley Common, why, that's fifteen miles away at least,' said David in dismay.

'That don' matter, we gotta go,' said Peter, excited that a week of frustration had ended – no matter how – with a definite lead. 'Can we have some money to go there, mum, an' have a scout around?' he asked, putting such appeal into his words that Mrs Reynolds could find no way to deny him.

'What does you aim to do?' she asked.

'Oh jus' look the place over, see what there is to be seen,' said David, taking up the cause.

'You won' go gettin' into no trouble, you two? I should say no, but it almos' safer to let you go than risk lettin' your dad get to know 'bout this place. He be sure to make terrible trouble if he go there. But you promise me: You leave any trouble-makin' to the police, eh?'

'Promise,' they both answered together.

CHAPTER FOURTEEN

Found

ON Berkley Common two West Indian boys were very conspicuous; Peter and David were self-conscious as they stepped off the bus before the village pub and the general store, where there were a good number of people about. The village was very open, with large houses widely spaced around three sides of a huge stretch of green. The boys attracted some searching looks that were embarrassing to them, not because they were unfriendly, but because they would have preferred to pass unnoticed on this particular journey. The important thing was to find the place quickly, and try to get out of sight.

'Can you see anythin'?' David asked, as they stood hesitating before the shop, under the scrutiny of eyes from all directions.

'Don' know what I lookin' for, man!' Peter answered.

'Well, "White Bricks" must mean somethin'. Look for those.'

And at once Peter saw a gateway that had a brick pillar at each side with white bricks placed regularly in the pattern. 'There!' he said, nodding towards the place at the opposite corner of the green. The house stood at the end of the row, with open heathland beyond it rising towards a wood. 'We gotta walk up this side right up to that wood, then work our way across till we top side of that place. Come on.' He led the way past all the houses and straight on across the rougher ground beyond, picking a route among gorse bushes and tiny outcrops of rock until they reached the shelter of the plantation of conifers on the shoulder of the hill. Here, once over the wall they did not continue on up to the ridge, but turned right alongside the wall, and sought a way to bring them in viewing distance of 'White Bricks'.

The trees were not a sufficient cover in themselves, but though the wall was only high enough to hide you if you crawled, the floor of the plantation was thickly overgrown with fern, and the fronds were high enough for the boys to push their way through standing, and to remain unseen from below. They started to traverse the slope, staying just inside the wood and keeping the common and the village in sight all the way.

It was exciting work; the cover was so good that they found it difficult to go forward; the unseen floor was uneven and treacherous with mouldering branches, while the fern resisted their progress, but cushioned them yieldingly when they stumbled.

The wood edge trespassed more on the heath as they advanced, so that, by the time they had reached a position from which they could see the back of the house, the wood wall and the boundary fence ran together. They continued further along the wood's edge until they were in a favourable position to see straight into the wire enclosure.

Here, behind the house and its outbuildings, was a training ground made out as a dog-track, though it had none of the frills of the real thing. Two men with a mechanically operated hare – a much posher affair than their old bike – were exercising a number of dogs that seemed to be doing circuits in threes. David counted six dogs in all. There was a black brindle, an all-black dog, and a black with white patches – these three were standing by. Running at the moment were two fallow dogs and a grey.

David looked at Pete, fearing to commit himself from this distance, though he was pretty sure that the black dog wasn't Jet. He couldn't have said why except that it didn't stand right. Pete didn't look excited, but of course he never did; he wouldn't give anything away until he was certain. 'Pity that dog isn't him, Pete,' David ventured, 'you could do your whistle an' he'd be here like a shot.'

'Yeah!' Peter said sadly. 'Fence or no fence.'

'Do you think he could jump it?' David asked, looking doubtfully at the very considerable wire fence that bounded even their side of the enclosure. He hadn't really meant that about the whistle; it was only a clever way he'd thought of to find out what Pete's ideas were about the black dog.

'They goin' to run the others now,' Pete said, and the man who held the dogs on short leads began to make his way round to the start, where a set of traps were fixed. As he approached and came up to the nearest point of the bend, David clutched Pete's arm impulsively.

'Hey!' he cried in excitement, 'that the G.P.O. man with long hair I talk to.'

'You sure, man?' Peter asked doubtingly.

'Sure! He even wearin' the same shirt, an' look at his hair – long like I say.'

'Well, if you quite sure ...'

136

'It mean Chamberlain must be connected with the break-in an' that Jet most probably here!'

By this time the man had walked the dogs round to the traps, and was busily putting them in to run. The other man had walked round the other way with the other dogs, and David noticed for the first time that there was a third man in a little hut that was the control room for the hare. He recognized Mr Chamberlain.

The hare started again, and the brothers gave it only a casual glance, for they were both looking beyond the track towards the outbuildings behind the house. Somewhere there, perhaps, Jet was hidden away. How did they get there?

The traps were sprung, and again their attention was caught as three dogs leapt out and started to race round the track. Even with their minds fixed on the problem of getting inside there was something about the race that compelled them.

David thought it was seeing dogs running from such a distance – they were so tiny, so effortless in movement when you couldn't hear their feet beating the turf or the panting sounds of their exertion. But it wasn't that.

The dog out in front was a long way ahead before they had run half a lap, and it was increasing its lead all the time. Well, that proved the black dog wasn't Jet, because that was last of the three, running two lengths behind the brindle and about eight lengths behind the black and white.

> Day is white.
> And black is the night.
> Ever'thin'...

David thought, and like lightning he snapped, 'Do your whistle, Pete,' as the dogs entered the second lap, running at this moment towards them. But somehow, Pete's whistle sounded as if in response to David's thought rather than his words, as if Pete already knew.

Pete stumbled out of hiding, mounted the wall that ran parallel on their side of the wire, and put everything he had into a second whistle.

The black and white dog shot off at a tangent from the track – there was no outside rail – and ran straight across towards them, streaking still like an arrow. But at the fence he stopped sharply and fussed backwards and forwards inside the wire, showing his delight.

The men, all three of them, were already coming at the run from different directions towards him, everything else abandoned.

'Come now, boy. Come up, over there,' Pete called, his voice coaxing. The dog became more excited, and moved back and forth, making little whining sounds in answer to Pete's voice and knee slapping. The men were getting nearer; the danger grew.

'Now, boy, here! Come over!' Pete called again.

First backing off, the dog suddenly bounded forward and leapt the fence straight into Pete's arms. The force of his flight knocked Pete backwards off the wall into the fern, and David rushed forward to help them up. But Pete, still holding the dog by the collar, scrambled to his feet. 'Go man, go back!' he cried, and started running back the way they had come.

David now took the lead to tread down the fern and give Pete an easier route, for the thick fern and the unevenness made it slow progress with the dog. The men were now up to the wire and kept pace with them easily, though they were reluctant to attempt the fence and an immediate capture. They were content yet to watch for the boys' next move.

When they came to the corner of the enclosure Pete and David jumped over the wall out of the wood onto the edge of the heath. Now Pete was able to release the dog, and they made a bee-line, running as fast as they could, diagonally over the open ground towards the bus-stop at the opposite corner. Both of them knew that it was essential to get back to a place where there were people before they were captured by Chamberlain and his men.

David looked round and saw that one of the men, the long-haired one, was scaling the wire, while the other two were moving fast down the line of the fence towards the house. He and Pete had a long, hard run before them if they were to reach safety before they were caught.

Thump! David heard the sound of the man's landing over the wire. They had about twenty yards start. He just ran behind Pete, dodging gorse bushes and stones, seeing Jet ambling along beside them enjoying it as a game. He could hear the thud of their pursuer's boots sounding steadily behind them. The man didn't shout, and he didn't flag; he came on relentlessly, knowing the desperate need to catch them.

With a quick glance over his shoulder David saw that the man had gained, he was five yards up on them. If that meant he was faster, it all depended on how much of a stayer he was. 'I mustn't look round again, I might stumble,' David thought. He concentrated on his running, and it felt harder; he was

gasping for breath, and his legs were hot and aching. He could feel that his speed was falling off from what he willed it to be. Perhaps his pursuer had gained another five yards; he yearned to turn round, to know his fate.

Jet frolicked along between him and Pete, and the dog's leisurely pace sustained because it shamed him. The urge to catch up with Jet kept David going, and just as the pounding footsteps behind seemed to be closing on him, they began suddenly, rapidly, to recede. David allowed himself a glance over his shoulder and he saw the man barely running at all, but staggering with exhaustion, his mouth agape. He had fallen a healthy distance behind.

But the temptation to relax, though strong, was dangerous. The men who had run towards the house had equipped themselves more suitably for the pursuit, and now came roaring out of the white-bricked gateway at dangerous speed in a land-rover. There was no racing against a car – even Jet would need to take that seriously; but they had covered some ground, they were nearing the bus-stop and the busy shop. Yet the car roared down the road, turned the corner, and came along the second side of the green, converging on them as they neared safety.

Spending precious breath David shouted: 'Run into the shop, Pete!' Peter made no answer, but his direction was right, and he ran harder to keep the way clear before the car arrived.

The car had hardly crunched to a stop on the gravelled track that surrounded the green before the doors were open and both men had leapt out. They set themselves purposefully between the boys and the shop, so that David saw they must dodge if they were to reach their objective.

Pete had no difficulty; he turned suddenly from his direct course, dodged round the back of the car, and disappeared from sight. David ran straight into the arms of Mr Chamberlain. As he gripped fiercely at the one boy's coat-sleeve, Mr Chamberlain followed with more interest the disappearance of the other boy and the dog into the shop. His men had followed to the door, and waited hesitant there for instructions. But no sooner had Pete rushed into the shop than he was bustled out again with Jet at his heels, and the shopkeeper behind them shouting angrily: 'How many times must I tell you: No dogs allowed! Can't you read the notice?'

He would have turned again, back to his customers, but David shouted desperately: 'Wait! Mister!' And when Mr Chamberlain tried to clamp a fat hand over his mouth, he struggled clear to arm's length – though not free – and shouted: 'Help! Help us!'

The shopkeeper stood; Peter backed away from Chamberlain's men; and David knew he had to make the shopkeeper and as many others as possible hear their plight. 'They stole our dog. He's worth thousands of pounds. We've just ... Get the police. Please get the police.'

The shopkeeper tutted as though the boy was mad or playing some silly game; he was about to turn again into his shop when an old lady whom he had been serving appeared behind him in the doorway and asked what was happening. When she heard she pushed her way out of the shop and simply stood on the pavement. With both her hands she beckoned them to come close, and they moved, promptly obedient, to make a half circle round her, such was her air of authority.

'You can let go of that boy,' she said to Mr Chamberlain, 'he doesn't look as though he wants to run away. Now, boy,' she said when David was free, 'what are you making all this noise about? I am a Justice of the Peace, and when the peace is broken it is my job to find out why and try if I can to mend it.'

'They stole our dog –' David began.

'Did you see them?' the lady asked sharply.

'No, but – '

'Your dog was stolen. Begin at the beginning.'

'Our dog is goin' to be a famous greyhound. He's won a lot of races. One morning I saw him' – David pointed to the long-haired man – 'pretending to mend telegraph wires near our house. Two days later the dog was stolen from its kennel in the night. The lock was taken off the door. We told the police. My dad suspected that he' – pointing to Mr Chamberlain – 'might be the thief because he knew about our dog and tried to buy it from us. We, me an' my brother, came up here to spy. We saw them trainin' dogs. Jet was one of them. My brother whistled an' he ran to us an' jumped the fence. They chased us down here.'

'Is that all?' the lady said.

'They put white patches on him with dye or somethin',' David said. 'An' – the G.P.O. van was stolen. The police told us.'

'Well, that is a complete story. What have you to say?' she turned to Mr Chamberlain.

'One of my men saw this dog on the common here. He was obviously lost and distressed, and we took him in. When he was rested we gave him a spell of exercise and found he could run a bit. We'd just started to realize he was valuable when these boys appeared and whistled the dog away. Of course we gave chase and – here we are.' Mr Chamberlain didn't sound at all guilty as he told his story. For a moment David doubted what he knew to be the truth.

'You reported finding the dog, of course?' the lady asked.

'Well, no. We were going to do that, naturally, when we realized how valuable he was.'

'You found him – when?'

'Yesterday.'

'And the white patches?'

'They were on him.'

'Did you know this valuable dog was missing?'

'Well, no, not really.'

'He did, 'cos the police told us they'd made routine inquiries at his place,' David said.

The lady looked at him keenly, and then she turned to Mr Chamberlain for an explanation.

'Well, you see, I didn't think much about that, to tell you the truth, and of course, knowing their dog was black, I didn't connect this one with theirs.'

'You didn't think someone might have painted patches on it?'

'No.'

'Well, that's all I need to know. We must tell the police at once. Mr Brookes,' she turned to the shop-keeper, 'will you phone the police and tell them the missing greyhound seems to have been found and is at Miss Armstrong's house? You don't dispute the boys' ownership, I suppose?' she asked Mr Chamberlain.

144

'I don't know who the owner is.'

'But you are not?'

'I never claimed I was.'

'Then you will have no objection to my relieving
you of the care of it. One of you boys can carry my
basket if you will, and we will go and have a cup of
tea and wait for the police to arrive. I think you had
better ask Mr Brookes to give you a nice, stout piece of
string so that you can keep that dog safe. We don't
want him to be lost or stolen again.'

David thought how funny it was that this little old
lady could order everybody around; and as they
walked slowly along beside her he was very impressed
to see the three big men turn sullenly but meekly
away, and climb into the land-rover to drive back to
'White Bricks', no doubt to patch up their story.

CHAPTER FIFTEEN

The Willow Cup

But the story they told is not part of this one. They were brought to justice and the Reynolds, and David in particular, had their parts to play in the affair. The penalties when they came shocked Mr Reynolds by their lightness, and he and David felt before the end of the case that they might have been on trial themselves for all the inconvenience it caused them. It was fortunate that at the same time exciting and worth-while things were also happening in their lives.

The white gradually wore out of Jet's coat, and he was unaffected by his adventure as far as his performance on the track was concerned. He soon returned to training and to competition, and was now famous throughout the country. He won every race that was worth winning in the Midlands, and was now up in London showing his class in really big competition and making the racing world sit up. Mr Reynolds was ready to launch him this season in the top races of all: the Greyhound Classics.

'Do you know somethin', Pete?' David said as they fed Allegro and both felt the absence of Jet.

'What?' Pete asked.

'When Jet was gettin' better from his illness an' seemed to take such a time over it, I was pleased to know he was always there an' we could play with him.'

Peter looked at his brother with interest, and this

146

encouraged David to go on. 'You know, I don' mean I
was glad he wasn't well or anythin', but I really got to
know him like when he was a puppy – you know what
I mean?'

'Yeah, he too often away now, man, an' we don' see
him.'

'An' when he here ever'thin' have to come second to
his trainin' an' safety. Since he was stole I never seen
such a carry-on.'

'I know. Dad start fussin' to be sure his food's all
right, an' he always there watchin' him like a hawk.
He even got a gun.'

'He say he goin' to put me on guard with it when
Jet come here to stay long time.'

'When that goin' to be, I wonder?' Peter said tartly.

'Yeah, an' what a pity people should want to steal
him anyway. I mean – that man with the long hair –
he seemed O.K. There somethin' about Jet that
change people.'

'I reckon they all wants a share in him.'

'That the trouble with gifts; you can't really say
they your own, other people think they have as much
right in them as you have.'

'Still, what we wants to see is Jet become a champion dog,' Peter said in a changed, more business-
like voice, as though they were being disloyal in what
they said. 'We just gotta help him best we can.'

'Yes,' said David sadly, 'but I wish champions
didn't have to be so special. It like havin' new clothes:
you wants to have 'em but you has to be so careful you
can' really enjoy them.'

Mrs Reynolds wasn't entirely happy either. She was
overwhelmed by all the money Jet was winning, and,

though she was very pleased to have a bit extra to help with the things they needed, she didn't know at all how to cope with thousands of pounds. 'I have wondered all the time about this dog,' she said. 'I try to decide what goin' to happen in the end; he have put a complete spell on your dad an' he can think of nothin' else. What you think goin' to happen if he win all these big races?'

'I dunno, but he have got to win them,' Peter said.

'Why does he have to? Haven't he won enough already?'

'No, 'cos he a wonder dog.'

'Yes, a wonder dog, an' the end of every race goin' to be known before it start. An' all this money goin' to keep on rollin' in that we don' know what to do with. An' your dad goin' to become more an' more this other man who think of nothin' but that one dog.'

'Yes, but we make a lot of fuss of Allegro, mum,' said David.

'I know you do. I'm glad. Allegro have to run her heart out to win, but Jet ain't like that, he jus' flies home, an' every time he bring me mo' money.'

And that was just the point, David thought. There was something frightening about this gift to the family, as they had always called Jet; he was like the cooking pot in the story that wouldn't stop making porridge. He himself was gifted with speed; he made all the other dogs look silly; and there seemed no end to it.

The television was switched on half an hour before the start of the weekly sports programme, and they all sat round pretending to watch the comedy show that

148

was usually so funny. David looked at his mother and saw the strain in her face; it was a strain that had come there since Jet had entered this crucial phase in his career when he was competing in the most important races: the Classics.

During the last six months Mr Reynolds had been travelling back and forth with him from London. They were all infected with anxiety and strain in this period, and in his mother's face David saw expressed something like the steel tension that was in the dog himself. Jet's will to win made him seem like a machine, or perhaps like some kind of natural force. You could feel nothing for him when he was involved in racing, for he was like lightning, like electricity: a cold, ruthless perfection. And all of them, the whole family, had become the servants of his will.

The comedy programme ended, and they all shuffled in their seats to try to relax as the titles of the programme were flashed on the screen. Then there was music, and short extracts from the next week's viewing; it seemed endless.

At last came the sports programme, its familiar music, and the familiar face of its introducer. He told them that the big event of the evening was to be the Greyhound Willow Cup in which the amazing greyhound, Jet, was competing, in an attempt to round off his tremendous year of success on the track. But first, they would be going over to watch some A.B.A. boxing, to see fights in the match between England and Ireland, which had reached an interesting stage.

No one in the Reynolds family shared in that interest, and Pete turned down the sound. They all sat, nervous and impatient, as two unknown flyweights battered away at each other in the ring. It was like something happening in another element: a glass-sided fish-tank.

But at last it was over; the familiar face returned, and they heard with relief that it was now time to go over to the White City where the dogs were out for the walk-around before the 1976 Willow Cup. The cup itself, he told them, was worth one thousand pounds, and there was a money prize of two thousand five hundred pounds as well. Then he introduced the dogs in the race as they had been drawn. Dogs, he said, that were of the very highest spirit, speed and racing quality.

'And finally, in lane six, the dog that has burst on the racing scene this season like a flash of lightning, or a thunderbolt. It is hard to find words to describe the effect this dog has had, because nothing like it has ever been known on the greyhound racing track. The black dog, Jet, winner of all the races that are worth winning; and winner with an ease that seems to show contempt for the very best in the field. Jet runs today in the outside lane, a disadvantage that I'm sure will affect him not at all. He has won all the Classics so far this season; can he add this one last win to complete the grand slam? Soon we shall know the answer.'

The camera meantime had been focused on Jet as he walked calmly, somehow as if he were dreaming, just ahead of his handler, the lead slack. His muzzled head was held high, and was precisely defined by the lights. At moments his blackness melted into the pool of shade – he had now lost all trace of white – and these moments of invisibility, when he seemed to lose substance and become part of the element of air and darkness, strengthened that sense you had of a creature unfettered by the laws of nature.

There were views of the track, the bookmakers busily at work, the crowd excitedly jostling for places, and over it all the commentator giving statistics and pedigrees. But at last the dogs were placed in the traps, and a silence fell on the stadium that was broken only by the commentator saying quietly, in awe: 'The Willow Cup, 1976.'

The hare sped silently away; but the effect was subdued, not at all like the moment on the local track when an electric hum shook the whole stadium. David missed the excitement of that: the friction of the mechanism, the driving power, and the surge of motion.

But past the traps the hare came streaking down the rails of the straight. As one, the traps shot open, and the six dogs came like bullets from guns. But the course of these bullets was not even; the one outside, which was the black dog, began to bend relentlessly over before first one and then another, a third and a fourth of those dogs inside him, until at the first turn he was running neck and neck with the dog in the inside lane.

'Whirlwind has held to the bend, but O what a cruel lot of advantage Jet has eaten away from the others – and here at the bend they are still coming – Pearl Tango's well up – but it's Whirlwind from Jet, now neck an' neck round the bend – it's Whirlwind holding – between these two – into the straight it's Jet going away with it – a length…' The commentator was going like a machine-gun himself, trying to describe what was almost too fast for the eye.

The camera followed Jet closely now; he was going like a comet, the rails flashing by in a blur on his inside. He held his ears flat to his head, and his black body sped like a beam over the ground, seeming to make no contact with it, as if his power came from inside himself.

It was a race no longer; the commentator was interested only in Jet's race against the clock. Was it a new track record? Round the second bend Jet's lead was two lengths, and that wasn't enough, because he was inching further and further out in front. It was three lengths now. The watchers in the Reynolds's living-room lost some of their tension – it was the same familiar story. Anyone who had been fool enough to suppose that Jet's form wouldn't hold was going to be disappointed along with those splendid, spirited dogs who followed, straggling in his tail.

Jet took the last turn, and the smooth flow of his action seemed more effortless on the television screen even than that of the hare. Which of these had the power that was greater than muscle and spirit could muster; was it the flop-eared, yellow parody of a hare, or was it this silent, black streak, Jet?

'... and Jet comes home ...' the commentator was saying when there was a loud report, audible over all other noise, and just beyond the finishing line Jet was enveloped momentarily in darkness; the blackness at the centre of the track seemed to advance suddenly upon the light and steal its place. 'The blackness of Obeah!' thought David, in sudden fear.

At the line the other dogs swerved away to the outside of the track; and, as they all came out from blackness into light, Jet was still ahead; but his motion

152

was somehow disturbed. He had taken on a wobble which grew to a stagger, so that he could not sustain his impetus. He suddenly proved that he did have legs and that they could no longer keep him up; for he went down on his nose, somersaulting over, and sliding joltingly to a stop. The other dogs went on past him, they too losing their rhythm, but drawing smoothly to a halt as the hare had done already. Before anybody could enter the track to go to him Jet was on his feet and limping with his tail close between his legs, going aimlessly down the track, away from the blackness.

'Oh dear! What can it be?' Mrs Reynolds cried in distress.

'There was a flash,' said David.

Now they listened.

'... the dog's owner, I think, yes, the owner is on the track. He has quieted the dog and seems to be examining him. Well! What a finish! It seemed that just as Jet was crossing the line a light ahead of him went wrong; it seemed to explode, and all I can suppose is that it put him out of his stride. What a thing to happen! And Jet had just broken every record in the book.'

'Now we have some information,' the man's voice continued, as the camera followed Mr Reynolds's activities. 'It seems that a light bulb did burst just ahead of Jet as he finished, and the fragments of glass showered down in his path. We can only hope that he has suffered no serious injury. What a tragedy for the sport that would be! But as yet, I can tell you no more.'

The camera showed Mr Reynolds picking Jet up in his arms. He carried him off the track and out of sight.

153

CHAPTER SIXTEEN

The Black Dog

Once upon a time when the story ended happily,
a new story began.

IT was six months later. The deep cut Jet had received
in his left forepaw was healed, and his speed was in no
way impaired; he was as fast as ever.

In the season that ended with the Willow Cup he
had carried off all the prizes, and he had established
records at tracks all over the country that would be a
terrible challenge to owners and dogs for years to
come. Some said there could never again be such a
dog.

Mr Reynolds had made a small fortune, and he had
no need to count upon those brave but modest little
successes Allegro had made on the track. Indeed,
Allegro was living now in honourable retirement as a
family pet. And now that Jet was famous, and an
undisputed champion, they could go on making
money even if he never set foot on the race-track
again. Already Mr Reynolds had opened a stud-book
and Jet had fathered several litters of puppies. Owners
everywhere were willing to pay to breed their dogs
from him, and, if it had been simply a question of
money-making, Mr Reynolds said, there was no better
way.

'What we need more money for, when we don'

know what to do wi' the money we got?' asked Mrs Reynolds.

'I thought we were goin' back to Jamaica,' David said, already doubting, but learning quickly from the silence with which the remark was received that this was not his parents' intention.

'There no hurry,' his dad said at last. 'Now we can afford we goin' to have a bran' new house with ever'thin' modern fo' your mum; we goin' to have our own car, an' just ever'thin' we needs. Pete have got that job at the Greyhound Stadium an' I can set up now in my own business. Ever'thin' goin' to be all right.'

'Yes, dad, but ...'

'You an' Lotty is doin' well at school; what we want to go leavin' it all for now ever'thin' come good?'

'But I thought you wanted to go back to your own life an' the family?' David said. 'Mum does.' He looked at his mother for support.

'Yes, we goin' back sometime – soon. But now things is easy, like your dad say. We wants to make the most of the chances we got. I goin' to start at the teachers' college nex' September as well,' his mother answered, but he wasn't convinced that she was sincere; she looked a bit sheepish.

'But I want to go back!' he persisted.

'Well, we can have a holiday at home,' Mr Reynolds offered, 'we can go every year – ain't nothin' to stop us.'

And David knew it was no good arguing; they weren't ready to go back. He knew that their talk of returning to Jamaica was only make-believe. England had something more to offer them in the way of comforts and luxuries like the house and the car, things that you could buy with money. But he *did* want to go back; it was not make-believe with him; and when he was able, when he was a man, he *would* go back and work in Jamaica; he would go home.

David thought about this a lot when he and Pete went out to the park with the dogs. Pete was happier now that he had his job; but David knew from the way that he talked about Jamaica – and he talked of it more often since their wealth had made the return possible – that he missed it too. When they were men they would go back together, and perhaps Lotty would want to go with them. In a way that would be like what Jet had done: he had decided something firmly, and would not be dissuaded from it. Jet must be a Jamaican at heart.

Since his accident in the Willow Cup, the dog had simply refused to race. They had tried him several times on the track, and, though the instinct to follow the lure was still strong enough to bring Jet bounding out of the trap after the hare, he had no sooner established his usual lead than he slowed, veered away to the outside, and stopped, letting the other dogs run on past him and away. Each time then he had slunk off the track with his tail between his legs, obviously afraid.

David remembered how Jet was enclosed by darkness when the light had burst, how it had seemed to advance from the black middle of the stadium that he thought of as Obeahland. Was Obeah a real power, the power behind Jet perhaps, and his gift of speed? Was Jet Obeah's gift to the family? And had Obeah helped them to be successful by advising his dad on

156

those two occasions when he had gone to the old house?

It was tempting to think so, for you could make the Obeahman's words fit the events. No doubt his dad believed in the magic; but there was too much of his mother in David, and he couldn't be convinced. The words the Obeahman had spoken would fit anything you wanted to believe – that was their only power. Jet was a very special dog who had come to them by chance, and then, when he had achieved his inevitable success, he had been scared off racing by his accident. That was what David decided; that was what he believed; doubts slid only occasionally into his mind.

And it was on occasions such as this, when Jet streaked back towards them with Allegro at his heels, that David had those doubts, those strange feelings. Jet came carrying the ball that Pete had thrown; he was enjoying the game as much as the boys. Pete tried to take the ball from him and Jet, teasing, backed away and bounded, growling with a pretence of defiance, as Pete went clumsily after him.

David seized the ball which Jet suddenly dropped at his feet, and with a 'Fetch it!' he hurled the ball as far down the field as he could. Both dogs went off like deer. David and Peter stood and watched the familiar yet still incredible motion as Jet sped away from them. He overran the ball and Allegro took it upon the second bounce. She stopped, turned neatly, and came streaking back to drop the ball at Peter's feet.

Jet wheeled, making a huge arc, and, seeing that he was out on his own, he put back his ears and sped, straight as an arrow, to come to them. In that brief burst of unmatchable speed, David wondered not only

157

at the power but at the nature of this dog. 'Knowing,' his dad had said of Jet, and it was tempting to believe that there was more to him than an accident on the track could explain. But now he stood before them, his eye alight, his tongue lolling lazily as he breathed: Jet, the black dog, eager at play.